The Vampire's Curse

S.J. Wright

For Kimmey, Debbie, Bethy, Angie, Brenda and Susan

Sisters are a treasure without measure

ACKNOWLEDGMENTS

There are a great many people who helped contribute towards the creation of this book. My family has been so supportive and wonderful throughout this process. Although my husband and I don't always agree about everything, he is the real reason that I was able to stay at home and write. Yes, I'm a stay-at-home mom. It's one of the hardest jobs in the world, but being able to stay home to take care of our son with special needs is a privilege. It also allowed me the time I needed to start working on the career I'd dreamed of since I was a little girl. So thank you, Duane. You helped make all this happen, and I will never fully be able to repay you for all the love, support and trust that you've given me.

Big hugs and thanks to my Mom and Dad, Brenda and Skeeter, Erin, and my always-dysfunctional sister Debbie (still miss you). Thanks also to my amazing in-laws, Judy and Stan, who are the best grandparents EVER!

Thank you also to Cameron and Devan for putting up with a mom who spends too many hours in front of her laptop at the kitchen table, jumping up every three minutes to pick up dropped food, let the dog out and move the laundry from the washer to the dryer.

CHAPTER 1

October 5, 2010

This is my first entry in the journal that has changed my life. I am not the first to write in it, but I very well may be the last. My name is Sarah Wood. I am 23 years old, and I have spent my whole life in a little town in Brown County, Indiana. My family (what is left of it) owns 22 acres outside of town. Most of the land is forest-covered hills, gorgeous and thick with white oak, beech, and dogwood trees. We have a large farmhouse that has been converted into a 5-bedroom inn. We have a large family cabin and two smaller cabins on the property as well.

We also have nine vampires. Yeah, I know. It sounds crazy. But it's true and still blows my mind when I think about it. So many things have happened since I discovered the vampire curse that has been holding my family captive for generations. Bad things.

I grew up believing that my mother had died in a car accident when I was just a little girl. I found out a few weeks ago that was a lie. Sort of. She really was dead, but not from a car accident. If it had only been that, then I would not be feeling like such a complete reject. Worse than that, I feel like everything I had always believed about myself was a fabrication. It may sound horrible, but I wish she had died that way. I would rather know that she was truly dead, rather than have to think about what she is now.

My Mom is a vampire. It was her choice. She hadn't loved her family enough to stay with us. She wanted out so badly that she chose to be a vampire. When I found out the truth, I wanted absolutely nothing to do with her. Unfortunately, she decided to come back into our lives.

Using a pair of crutches borrowed from our doctor, I hopped to the front door, checked that it was locked, and did the same to the back door before heading very slowly up the stairs. My right ankle had been sprained earlier that night. I guess I was lucky that I had gotten away with just a sprain, considering that there had been one hell of a battle and one of my friends, Alex, had nearly died. Technically, he *was* dead. Actually, more like undead.

It had fallen on my shoulders to decide whether Alex should be turned into a vampire. He had sustained a horrific injury when a rogue vampire had attacked him. With his blood pooling beneath him in a crimson circle, I sent my friend back into a world that he had hated. And I hated myself for sending him there.

I paused in the hallway by my sister's room. Katie's door was closed and the light was out. I hesitated beside it, wanting to see how she was doing. Raising my hand in preparation to knock gently on her door, I hesitated. She had been through a lot over the last few days. First, she had to hear me tell the truth about our mother leaving us. Then she was kidnapped by a group of vampires who wanted to use her as bait to try to get me to release one of their kind that was in the containment field.

That was another revelation that had shocked me to no end. As it turned out, my father and his father before him and five more generations of our family had been responsible for the vampires that were on our property. According to the journal that my grandfather had passed down to me, back in the early 1800's, a Pawnee ancestor of my father's conducted a tribal ceremony on our land that effectively sealed out supernatural creatures and could hold vampires within. Only the eldest sons of our direct family line had the power necessary to invite a vampire in or release one. It was intended to be a peaceful resting place where vampires could go and not be worried about being attacked while they enjoyed what they called "the long sleep." However, when my father and mother failed to produce a son, the role fell to me. Hooray.

I sighed and turned from Katie's door. Disturbing her sleep would not be helpful. We could talk in the morning. My ankle was throbbing and I was completely exhausted after everything that had happened. All I wanted to do was climb into bed, throw the covers over myself, and sleep without interruption.

I hobbled into my bedroom and closed the door as quietly as I could. Then I turned towards my bed.

"Hello, Sarah."

My breath caught painfully in my chest, and I swallowed a cry of alarm when I saw the familiar face of the person sitting so calmly on my bed. I had thought the night could not possibly get any worse. Shows how wrong I was.

"Mom?"

My heart fluttered like a trapped butterfly. Sitting before me on my own bed was a person I thought had died many years ago, looking like she had not aged a single minute in the sixteen years since we had last seen her. She was dressed in a pair of stylish silk gauchos, three-inch glossy high heels, and a gorgeous silk top the color of ripe peaches. Her matching earrings, flashing in the meager light coming in from hall, dangled nearly to her shoulders.

There was a real difference in the set of her features that made her seem like something that did not belong here on earth. The perfection of her skin and the vibrant shine in her blue eyes gave firm evidence that this was not the same person who had given birth to me. There was a spark in her gaze that was entirely inhuman.

"What?" I stammered.

She smiled, "It's been a long time, sweetie."

Her voice was only subtly different, and the memory of it squeezed my heart and made me feel like I could not draw a real breath of air. Only shallow little gulps of oxygen sustained me as I stared at her. That was when the edges of my vision began to turn black. Heavy warmth assailed my stomach and flowed upward into my chest. My pulse began racing madly. The last thing I saw before I blacked out was my mother's face. I had one clear, concrete wish that I tried desperately to cling to as I fell into the darkness.

I really, really hoped that she would not be there when I woke back up.

"Sarah?" My sister Katie was hovering over me. I thought it was so pretty how the rays of sunlight played across the dark curls falling over her shoulders. Why did I have to end up inheriting my Dad's mild wavy mouse-brown hair and she ended up with that? It was not fair. Katie had also ended up with the intelligence to take her to the top of her high school graduating class and get into Purdue University's Veterinary Medicine program. However, given the ridiculously dramatic things happening in our home life, I doubted she would get a chance to finish school.

I groaned and rolled my eyes, "Oh, Christ. Please tell me she wasn't here. It was just a bad dream, right?"

"Who?"

I found that I was lying on the hard, polished wood of my bedroom floor. The sunlight from one window had fallen over me like a warm blanket, but my whole body was still stiff from lying on the floor all night. I gingerly propped myself up on my elbows and blinked.

"What happened to you?" Katie asked, regarding me with a doubtful stare.

"I think I fainted." I sat up and gripped her hands violently. "You didn't see anybody in the house last night, did you?"

"No. Let me go." She yanked her hands away, stood up and glared down at me. That look was like turning a page from the past. How many times had she flashed those dark eyes at me in irritated resentment? A hundred? A thousand?

I slowly got to my feet and rubbed the back of my neck. It hurt like a bitch. I debated telling my sister about who I had seen the night before. I was supposed to be the strong one, and after all I had witnessed that night, seeing my mother had evidently pushed me past my emotional threshold. There was no way I was putting that on Katie.

"Who did you see?" She asked, cocking her head to one side.

"Nobody. I think I just had a bad dream after I passed out or something." I shoved my hair out of my face and ground my teeth together. I just knew all this lying was going to end up biting me in the ass. She watched me for a few seconds, and I could see the questions flashing in her eyes.

"You make any coffee?" I asked, trying to deflect her.

She nodded. "I came in here to tell you it was ready."

"Thanks."

She hesitated in the doorway, her beautiful brown eyes somber. "We need to talk."

Using only one crutch, I managed to grab a clean pair of white cotton panties from my nightstand and my thick yellow robe from the hook inside my closet, "After my shower." Stopping for a second beside her, I reached out with my free hand and squeezed her arm gently, "Try not to worry too much. We'll get it worked out, Katie-bug."

She tore her gaze from me and turned her head indignantly, "Don't call me that. I'm not a little kid, Sarah."

That hurt. I drew a little painful breath and watched as she walked away. What happened to the little sister who used to be my best friend? Was it only that she was growing up? Maybe the good memories of home had begun to be tainted by all the crazy vampire stuff. It certainly made me want to run away sometimes. However, I did not want that to sever our bond and I needed to do something to make things better between us before it was too late.

After my shower, I examined my ankle. It was bruised, but felt a little better than it had the previous night. I decided to try to get around with just the single crutch. I got dressed and made my way slowly downstairs to the kitchen. Katie was pouring coffee for me, and I noticed immediately the iron set of her shoulders and the flare of annoyance in her eyes. She handed the cup to me.

"I can't stay here." She said. That was not surprising. She had become pretty good at running away lately.

"What about your Jeep?"

"I'll need a ride to the gas station up at 135 and County Line. That's where they…" Her voice cracked. Her eyes were darting around the room, vivid with fear, and she pressed her slender white fingers to her throat, "That's where…" Then the dam broke.

Shiny tears rolled from her eyes down her face and I folded her in my arms quickly. This was the kind of thing I had wanted to avoid. Luckily, her captors had not hurt her, but she was understandably traumatized after everything that had happened. She rested her head on my shoulder and I felt the wetness from her tears soaking through the fabric of my long-sleeved T-shirt. She sobbed quietly while I stroked the curls that draped down her back. There was a horribly warm ache in my chest as I tried to comfort her. I felt like I was partially responsible for her getting into all of this, and it chilled my blood to consider the possibility that she might have been killed.

"We're going to work it out." I whispered, "None of this should have happened to you. You shouldn't have ever been involved. I'm sorry, Katie."

She pulled away, tried to brush the tears from her face, and grabbed a tissue from the box of Kleenex sitting on the counter by the sink. I tried to think of anything I might do or say to make this whole thing less scary for her, but the words would not come. I did not want to lie. The vampires were not going anywhere.

With the sobs quieting and the tears slowing to a trickle, Katie's face looked drained and pale as alabaster. She wiped her nose and set her gaze on my face.

"What are we going to do, Sarah?"

"Not we. Me. You're going back to school." I replied evenly.

She rolled her eyes dramatically and dabbed at a few more tears, "How can I concentrate on classes when I know that all of this is going on here? Knowing how much danger you're in? And what the hell are they doing here anyway?"

"It's a really long story. I've got a journal that Grandpa Wood left for Dad."

11

Surprise flickered across her face, "That's the journal that Fleming brought?"

"Yes. And you can read it yourself. It explains a lot."

Her eyes narrowed, "Mom has something to do with all this, doesn't she?"

Hesitating, I poured the cream into my coffee and stirred it slowly, watching the colors mix as I tried to come up with some answer that would not send Katie into hysterics. I had no doubt that would be her reaction would be if I told her the truth.

"Sarah?"

I turned to her and spoke in a clipped tone, "I don't want to talk about her. Yes, she has something to do with this, but the vampires were here before she married Dad. Let's leave it at that. I seriously do *not* want to talk about her."

She was very quiet for a few minutes and then turned toward the door that led to the entryway, "So you'll give me a ride?"

"Yes. And you can take the journal with you."

Thirty minutes later, we were driving up towards Greenwood in silence. The sun had come out from behind some earlier clouds and I noticed for the first time that the leaves were beginning to change into the gorgeous yellow, crimson, and orange hues that signaled winter would soon be closing in. There was light traffic going north, but it seemed like the trip up there took forever with both of us being so unwilling to reveal what was going on in our heads. Only when we pulled up next to her Jeep at the gas station did she turn to me.

"I'm going to be checking in a lot, Sarah."

I nodded, staring straight ahead, "That's a good idea. I'll keep my cell with me, no matter what I'm doing."

"Love you, sis." With those words, she stepped out of my truck, got her bag from behind her seat, and shut the door.

I waited until she had started the Jeep and pulled away before I hung my head and started crying. My Dad would have been ashamed to see me at that moment, broken and beat down, sobbing in the quiet confines of my truck. I was supposed to be strong all the time—a rock that everyone else could lean on. I missed him so much. Wanting to please him had meant everything to me not so long ago. However, an increasing sense of animosity had seeped into my head over the years as I saw my childhood friends grow up and move away from the town. I was expected to stay and continue at the inn. And I had been doing just that, even though my soul raged against it. It was always Katie who was going to go off and do great things. Not me. I had a job already.

No wonder I was so angry all the time, I thought suddenly. My head came up slowly as an odd sort of peace settled inside my gut. Maybe there was a way out of this. What if I could sell the inn, the land and just move away and do my own thing? Hope, unfamiliar and sweet, swept through me. It was a lovely little gentle humming that moved through my veins very slowly, leaving me replenished and feeling a little stronger.

If I could sell and just get away, I might do anything. I could go to college. Maybe I could find a great guy, settle down somewhere, and have two and a half kids and a minivan. Shaking my head, I laughed a little at that thought and pulled away from the gas station. It was the idea of freedom that sparked my imagination. I did not really care what I ended up doing. I wanted to start my own life. Away from Woodhaven inn. Away from Brown County. That last thought made me hesitate. Maybe not that far away. That little doubt stayed with me as I drove south.

The rest of the way home, I tried not to think about any of it. I turned the volume up on the stereo, rolled the window down and sang along with John Mellencamp about Jack and Diane.

CHAPTER 2

When I pulled up by the front gate to open it, I saw Messenger. She was a gorgeous black Tennessee Walking horse and was one of only two horses that we kept on the property. After kicking down a gate the day before, she had been roaming the whole twenty-two acres at will because Alex and I had failed to catch her. I certainly was not about to try to mess with her while my ankle was still bothering me.

She had been grazing along the edge of the driveway about a hundred feet from the gate. When I hopped out of the truck with my crutch, she raised her head and fixed her wide intelligent eyes on me. I shook my head at her, opened the gate, and half stumbled back to the truck. She must have sensed she had an opening, because she began prancing over with her long silky tail flowing along behind her. I left the driver's door open and did not fasten my seatbelt, but drove right through, slammed it back into park and jumped out.

I got the gate closed just as she reached the truck. Grinning at her, I shook my head.

"No, you don't, little miss. And I will get you back into your pasture. You can be sure of that."

She tossed her head and reared up, then turned and loped off towards the woods.

"Stubborn bitch of a horse."

Still swearing, I got back in the truck and headed up to the house.

The rest of that day, I tried to keep myself busy around the house, but there was not much I could accomplish with my ankle all messed up. I did manage to get several loads of laundry done. About halfway through folding the last load, I realized I was running on fumes. I could not remember the last time I had gotten a decent night's sleep. After I finished folding the last of the laundry, I hobbled upstairs and put on my warmest flannel pajamas.

The plan was to make myself a sandwich and a cup of caffeine-free tea, watch a little of the evening news and then fall into my bed. As I was spreading a thin layer of mayonnaise on a slice of bread, there was a knock at the front door. I was damn sure it was not an encyclopedia salesman. Probably a vampire. Wonderful.

Maybe if I did not answer the door, the creature would go away. Wishful thinking. I laid the knife down and left the kitchen, swinging my crutch before me and made my way through the entry hall in my fluffy white house slippers and peered outside. A dark, familiar figure stood on the porch.

Michael. I groaned and unlocked the door.

He was the first vampire I had ever met. He was cool, sarcastic, and utterly gorgeous in a bad-boy sort of way. He was also, as far as I knew, totally attracted to me. The feeling was mutual. I had been able to avoid any serious physical entanglements with him so far, but I was sure that was not going to last very long. There was definitely a spark between the two of us that seemed to grow more alluring every moment we were within each other's sights.

Pulling the heavy wooden door open just an inch or two, I looked at him through the screen. The determined set of his jaw reminded me that we had a lot to discuss.

"We need to talk. You're going to have to invite me into the house, Sarah."

I snorted, "Yeah, like that's going to happen."

One of his dark eyebrows rose slightly in annoyance, "Would you rather come out here?"

"It's cold as a witch's tit out there tonight. I'm already in my pajamas."

"You know I won't hurt you. I'd suffer through a thousand days in the sun before I'd allow *anyone* to hurt you." He murmured with deep sincerity. I studied him. The smooth planes of his face were clear of any sarcasm. He was serious. Unwillingly, I felt a tiny smile beginning to form on my face.

"Prove it." However, I was still smiling. I could not help it. He had the most engaging little half grin on his face, and between that and his dancing blue eyes, I was bound to give in. I felt heat pooling in the pit of my stomach. He was right. We had a lot to discuss, and all my instincts told me emphatically that Michael would not attack me. Well, not in an effort to injure me. Any physical attack would more likely involve him removing my clothes first, which was not a threat to anything except my own personal sense of emotional stability.

Stepping back and pulling the door with me, I said lightly, "Please come in, Michael."

He pulled the screen door open and sauntered in, then firmly pushed the door closed and looked around doubtfully.

"Are you alone?"

"For now, yes," Hopping along with my one crutch, I headed into the den with its soft, casual earth-toned furniture and large television, sat on the plaid arm chair and put my injured ankle up on the matching ottoman. I crossed my arms over my middle and watched him carefully.

"Katie went back to school." I told him.

Instead of taking a seat on the long sofa, he stood at the windows, looking out through the wide wood blinds into the dark night. He looked delicious. He had dressed in a pair of dark jeans that fit him just right across his butt. He wore a long-sleeved gray fleece pullover and his rich brown hair had been recklessly styled. The dark waving locks still looked damp.

21

"Where do you shower?" I asked suddenly.

"That's an odd question, given everything that happened last night." He turned and cocked one dark eyebrow.

"I'm curious. About a lot of things."

He shrugged and turned, "Since you're so curious, I'll indulge you for now."

He lowered himself onto the sofa and crossed one ankle over his knee in a manly gesture, "Your father had indoor plumbing installed in the old cowshed about fifteen years ago. He was kind enough to have a shower put in."

The old cowshed had been designated a no-play zone by our Dad when we were growing up. Dad had said that there were tools in there that were not safe for kids to be messing around with. He had padlocked the doors to the shed early on, so Katie and I had never really attempted to get in there. I did know there was a loft there because above the main doors, there was a swinging door that was not locked.

I had not considered Michael's living conditions. I was oddly glad that my father had thought of it, though. Then I realized that there was something else that he probably needed.

"How do you get...?" I stammered.

"Blood?" He sent me another one of those half smiles that made my insides feel like they were turning inside out.

"Yeah."

"I'm a reasonably old vampire. I don't require much blood. What I do need comes from animals in the woods. It's not what I would prefer, of course."

Animal blood. Oh, well that was not so bad. Was it?

"I don't know whether to believe you or not." I said. It would have been so easy for him to lie to me at that point. However, as far as I knew, there were no unsolved murders in the area. I considered the possibility that he might be telling the truth.

"Human blood can be obtained. I was able to secure a regular supply from a blood bank several years ago, but unfortunately my contact there disappeared." He leaned forward; his clear eyes fixed on me with an intensity that made me draw a shaky breath.

I cleared my throat, "What happened with Alex?"

"Victoria drained him and then we both gave him our blood. It took awhile for him to come around, but he seems to be getting control of his faculties."

Bowing my head, I pressed my hands against my warm cheeks, "He probably hates me."

Michael's reply was not very comforting, "That's probably true. And it poses a bigger problem than we first thought."

"Why?"

"Because the containment field can't hold him as it does Victoria and I and the others."

That statement about Alex had me a little perplexed. Alex had been changed into a vampire within the field so it had no control over him? That *would* be a big problem, given the fact that the perimeter of the containment field was the only barrier we had against vampires and other unusual creatures. I was glad I had not seen a werewolf yet.

"How do you know?"

He hesitated, a deliberate frown creasing his beautiful mouth, "He got away from us. Crossed the boundary line and then came back."

I turned away from him, "And he's angry at me. Who told him that it was me?"

"Victoria. She wasn't trying to cause trouble."

An unladylike curse bubbled from my lips, "Bullshit."

Then I recalled seeing my mother before I passed out in my bedroom and my anger was swept away thoroughly by another stronger emotion. Turning to look at him again, I searched his face for any sign of consolation, "Michael, my mother is back."

He looked at me for a long moment, a trace of pity looming in the depths of his eyes, "I know. She came to see us. She sensed that Alex was in trouble."

"Why was she able to come into the house without an invitation?"

"How do you know she didn't get one?" He countered, tilting his head to one side and gazing at me expectantly. Oh, shit. Had Katie invited her in? I was sure that she would have mentioned that at some point during our conversations that morning.

"I think the containment field doesn't work for her either. She was turned within the field like Alex was." He said quietly, "It doesn't matter. Now that Alex is a vampire again, he's of no use to her as a guardian for you. I would imagine she'll probably take him back to California."

I was really hoping all she wanted was to take Alex back. With that thought, I began to feel like a coward.

I let out a breath, "I really hope so." However, I would still feel like I had taken the easy way out if that really did happen. I wanted my mother to be gone to save myself pain. I wanted Alex to be human again— to be my friend. I did not have very many friends.

"With Alex gone, you'll be unprotected." There was an honest concern in his tone and his mouth was pressed into an uncompromising line that reminded me strangely of an iron bridge. A bridge to nowhere. Evidently, he did not consider himself my protector.

Swallowing a fierce sadness, I bit out, "I don't want protection. I don't want anyone else getting hurt." My voice sounded snappy and defensive. I could have kicked myself for going overboard with the bad attitude.

I stared resolutely at the wall, hoping he did not sense the fear in me. Protection sounded great, but after what had happened to Alex, I was terrified to bring anybody else into this. My eyes snapped back to him.

"Did you find Luanna?" Luanna had been one of the rogue vampires that had been sent to us by the Council. Her mate, Gunter, had been the one who dealt the blow to Alex that effectively ended his life.

"Yes. We've managed to get only a little information out of her. We've got her contained for now in one of the larger caves under the meadow."

"What did she have to say?"

"That Gunter acted alone." His eyes flashed with annoyed rage, "I know she's lying, but I can't prove it."

"Would it help if I talked to her?"

"It may drive her mad, having a warm-blooded human so close. She hasn't fed for days, and she's much younger than I am."

"Well, talk to Victoria about it. If you both agree, then I'll try." I hesitated for a split second, realizing that would be a huge error on my part, "But I'm not going out there until my mother leaves. I don't want to see her."

He tipped his head back in exasperation and threw one arm across the back of the sofa, "You don't have anything to fear from Selena. She didn't come here to get back her old life, Sarah."

My hands clenched into tight knots as hot anger flooded my brain, "I am *not* afraid of her."

When he rose from his seat and moved towards me, I froze. Until that moment, I had not realized how small the room seemed to have become. With him there, the space appeared small, cramped, the furniture tiny and fragile. *Almost as fragile as I was.* The heat in my stomach began to come alive again, sending tickling little electric bolts into my arms and legs and then centering again low in my womb. I had felt desire in the past, but nothing compared to this thick rolling warmth that stole through me so deliciously. I felt perspiration begin to dampen my palms, but I tried to ignore it.

The tingling, mesmerizing heat blazed even hotter in my veins as I watched him stroll towards me. There was a blatant elegance in the careless way he moved, from the slight swing of his arms to the fluid action in his long legs. He leaned over me, his eyes cold and calculating, his cool breath swirled over my cheeks like a freezing winter mist.

"You're not afraid?"

I could not move. He was holding me prisoner without chains, without bars of any kind. He held me with the steady, penetrating focus of a hunter who will not be denied his prey. My fingers itched to touch him, to trail over his skin in slow gliding strokes. But he could not have me. No one could really have me. I could not let them. I could not let him.

Trying to gain any amount of control over the situation, and myself I gestured towards my injured ankle. However, I could not stop looking at his mouth, wondering how it would feel to have those lips locked with mine in a slick, demanding kiss.

"I would think you might try to be more of a gentleman. I do have a sprained ankle." I said weakly.

His striking blue eyes crinkled at the corners as he gave me a slow, sweeping smile. I saw a tiny vein in his jaw pulse and knew he was angry on some level. Nevertheless, any attention from a man that required me to give up any part of myself seemed totally wrong. Then again, what did I know? It was not as if I had ever been in a real relationship. I did not think that Trevor Kincaid counted because although we had sex couple times, it certainly was not a committed relationship. He had a girlfriend that I did not know about while we were seeing each other. Sweet, huh? Yeah, he was a real winner.

Michael tossed a dismissive glance over his shoulder at me and wandered back to the windows again. He leaned against the wall, his face turned away from me.

"Did Alex tell you about the Breath-Giver?" He asked.

I released the breath I had been holding back, "Yes, a little."

"I've been wondering what my chances would be if I asked her to change me back into a human as she did Alex."

"Oh." The idea of Michael being human was soul stirring. The possibilities stretched out before me like a dazzling parade. I envisioned him laughing beside me at the kitchen table, eating my French toast. I could see the two of us walking quietly together, hand in hand down the driveway to get the mail. Pretty pictures. But it was completely unrealistic, I reminded myself sternly. And I was still extremely skeptical of the whole "breath-giver" thing.

Alex had told me before he had gotten hurt that he used to be a vampire and then some strange unearthly creature turned him back into a human. Sounded too farfetched to me, but then again, I did not used to believe in vampires either.

Michael turned his head back towards me, "What price do you suppose she might ask for such a thing?" The timbre of his voice was ripe with vulnerability.

I watched the play of emotions cross his face. Hope. Frustration. Passion. However, I remained silent, fearing a return of those heartbreaking scenes that had played out in my head. There were more practical questions to ask. If Michael were human again, what would that mean to the Council? The vampire Council had sent him here because of some crime. If he were human, would they permit him his freedom?

"Why did they send you here? What did you do wrong?" I finally asked.

31

A mysterious grin lifted his lips, "They were afraid."

"So you didn't actually do anything wrong? They just fear you?" I refolded my arms across my chest and met his suddenly hostile stare calmly, "That sounds like a load of horse shit, if you ask me."

He shrugged slightly, "They wanted an excuse. They found one."

His muscular body turned my way, and he crossed the room in a few decisive steps. I noticed with a startling sense of awe that his eye color had changed. Instead of the crystal-blue hue that I had seen time after time, even in my dreams, his eyes were brilliantly silver and the dark brows arching defiantly over them were creased with tension. He grasped one of my hands, pulled it towards him, and turned it over.

"Michael…" I breathed his name like a prayer.

I watched, disbelievingly, as he pressed a fiery kiss into the palm of my hand. I had never before felt the alarming sensation of Michael's lips on my flesh. It was a moment I would not soon forget. Every other sensation in my body ground to a sudden and silent halt when I felt the warmth of his lips. It seemed as if every other part of my body had gone numb with the shock of it. But the palm of my hand was burning. A rolling heat made me gasp.

When I raised my head to look at him, all I saw was a blur of motion. He had moved so fast that I had barely realized he was leaving. I heard the backdoor open and the screen door squeak as he passed through to the back yard. Then a terribly cold silence fell over the room.

I looked at the hand he had kissed. There was nothing there. I had expected it to be blistered and red. Curling my fingers into the place where he had pressed his mouth, I leaned my head back against the armchair and sighed. It was a good thing that he had decided to be a gentleman. Because I was positive that the next time we were completely alone, I would not have the will to keep myself away from him. Stupid, sexy vampire.

S.J. Wright

CHAPTER 3

Katie kept her promise to stay in touch. She called shortly after Michael made his hasty departure. She sounded tired and understandably irritated, but the conversation was amicable, and I hung up thinking that she and I were on the same page. I did not tell her that our mother was back. I figured that the less my sister knew, the better off she would be.

When I finally climbed into bed that night and turned off the lamp next to me, I still felt very uneasy. I had been anticipating another visit from my mother with a sickening fear. Would she want something from me? What about Katie? My feelings for my mother had morphed into this blackened, lurking phantom that hovered inside my gut and pushed away common sense. It was a heavy burden that caused me to look at myself harshly. I recognized suddenly that I had few real friends. My father had trusted me to run the inn, but did not have enough confidence in me to encourage me to go to college. Was I even smart enough for college?

The self-doubt had begun to wear away the fragile threads of confidence that had sustained me for most of my life. I tried to push the dark tendrils of doubt out of my head. There was nothing wrong with me. I was a good person and capable of great accomplishment. Right?

I flung myself onto my back and pressed my fingers against my cheeks. I could not let this black cloud of self-hate saturate my brain anymore. I closed my eyes and tried to take some slow deep breaths. I am a great person, I told myself. I am worthy of being loved.

Then I heard a sharp, jarring tap on my window. I jerked back in surprise and stared at the window. What if it were Alex? Or my mother? Tentatively, I pushed the covers off me and put my feet on the floor. Another louder tap sounded, rattling the windowpanes.

With an impulsive burst of courage, I stepped to the window and yanked on the strings that brought the blinds up. I stared outside, but saw nothing at first. Without thinking, I unlocked the window and pushed it open. A bitterly cold rush of air assailed me as I stood there in my worn pink striped pajamas. The night outside was grimly silent except for the whistling of the wind through the window, and I shivered in trepidation.

A large human form rose up from the roof under the window, and I jerked back in surprise with my heart slamming in my chest.

"You weren't expecting me?"

A human form, perhaps. However, not human anymore. Alex had become something radically different from the easy-going, All-American guy that I had come to know. His golden hair was brighter, glistening like cold diamonds in the frigid night air, and his eyes were lit with emerald fire that seared every object he gazed upon. His powerful, stunning body balanced expertly on the balls of his bare feet and his hands settled firmly against the outside frame of the window with the lean angular muscles of his arms tensely bunched. He was barely dressed at all, only wearing a ragged pair of cut-off jean shorts.

I took another step back from the window and shook my head in denial, "Oh, God. Alex…"

Tears blurred the image of the creature before me. My friend was gone. An ache so profoundly painful struck me in the chest, pressed me back from the window and against the far wall of my bedroom.

"Let me in." His voice was low and sweetly melodic.

A frantic sob escaped my throat in response. The wind continued to pour through the open window, rattling the edges of the upraised blinds against the window casing. The only source of illumination was a single nightlight plugged into the wall by my bed, but it was enough.

"Look at me, Sarah." His voice was impossible to ignore, compelling in a way that even Michael's had never been.

I dashed the tears away with a shaking fist and blinked at him.

"You will let me in. *Now*."

The voice that answered was my own, but I felt completely separate from it. Any will of my own was lost to me, swept away by the unyielding force of his presence and the guilt that was ripping me into pieces.

"Come in." It was barely a whisper of sound. Some tiny little nothing that had the power of everything behind it, because the moment those words came from me, I knew my fate was set in stone. With a growing sense of awe, I watched him step through the open window and come across the room to stand before me like some golden god returning to the scene of his demise.

His expression was infused with determination, but when he bent down towards me, I saw the briefest, sweetest cloud of doubt pass over him. I had to snatch at that before it faded away and left me completely helpless. It was all I had. It was a reminder that somewhere beneath the skin of this dark soul, a fragment of the man I had known still flickered.

Reaching out with desperate hands, I cupped his fierce face.

"Tell me you're still there." It was a sad plea, accentuated by the hot tears that trailed down my face without pause.

His fiery eyes widened in surprise. He had expected fear or anger, not quivering supplication. He had never witnessed that side of me. I had lost my father and nearly lost my sister. Having to say goodbye to anyone else, especially a friend like Alex would change me. It might just destroy me. Grasping my hands within his own, he drew them away from his face and turned his head to the side.

"Say something." I whispered hoarsely, urgently, "Tell me you hate me."

Again, our eyes locked. Desire shot through me unexpectedly. Without another thought, only a savage need to have him back in any capacity, I moved forward and fastened my mouth on his. For just a tiny instant, he froze. All I wanted was to hold onto him, to keep him with me. However, somewhere inside, I felt the tide turning and began to understand that there was something infinitely separate from our friendship that had begun to flower inside of me.

His hard-muscled, bare arms stole around me as we both knelt there on the floor, our knees bent against the chill of the hard wood. I could feel the heat of his chest through my pajama shirt. Breaking away with a whimper, I tried to unbutton it, but my fingers were trembling violently. Realizing my intent, Alex simply wrenched the front of the shirt apart in his hands, the buttons popping off and falling to the floor.

It was not enough. Having his warm flesh pressed so closely against me, having his lips searching and teasing my own. It was not nearly enough. Our tongues met in a silken dance and still, I ached. With a low groan, he jerked away and rose to his feet, pulling me with him. In a flash and without a single whispered word between us, he spread me out upon the turned down flannel sheets of my bed.

The pressure of his fingers was painful against my skin, but it only increased the whirlwind of need spreading through me. Every time we touched each other, it was like a frantic race to find something else, to explore another sensation that might give us both some way to hold onto something that seemed to be flashing into nothingness.

At some point, he drew off my pajama bottoms and panties and left his shorts on the floor. There was a moment when doubt tickled at the edges of my mind, but it was swept away so quickly by the sweet urgency in his kiss and the way his strong hands trembled as he pushed my hair back from my face.

We were both mad with desire, desperate for the connection to be made complete. And when the moment came, and our bodies became one, we were left drowning in our passion for each other and our

41

faces were wet with tears. I watched, fascinated, as ruby drops fell onto my chest. His tears. I felt something break inside me at the sight. He moved hesitantly within me and I saw him close his eyes.

"Make it real," He murmured, "Not another dream. It has to be real this time."

I pumped my hips upwards sharply, feeling the length of him touch my core. And I fell apart all over again, splintering into a thousand scattered pieces. Everything I was and everything I thought I knew disappeared when Alex rolled his head back and growled in triumph.

His moment came and he gripped me with hands that felt like iron around my hips. Looking up at him, I could not collect my thoughts. His pure powerful release was animalistic and elemental, taking every emotion from the depths of him and sending it out into the universe. And it left him depleted.

When his eyes slid over me again, I saw some tiny warning in their glow. But I did not care. My own release had left me feeling languid, drugged. He could have jumped out of bed and done a jig at that point and I would not have batted an eye. Every muscle in my body was useless. So when he moved towards my neck with another kind of heated need lighting the emerald of his eyes, I did not move. I did not protest.

He could take what he wanted. My blood, my body, my soul. It seemed that I belonged to him in so many remarkable ways. I felt that, acknowledged it. And felt no need to stop him. To his benefit, he did press his feverish fingers against my face, forcing me to look at him directly in order to get an answer.

"Yes or no, sweet Sarah."

I nodded slowly and opened myself completely to him. No matter what he wanted, it was his tonight. His mouth traced a path of scorching kisses from my ear, along my jaw and down to my neck, where he used his tongue and the heat of his warm wet mouth to ignite this newly discovered passion yet again.

By the time I felt those two tiny pinpricks against my skin; he had slid inside of me again and was quickly pushing me back up into the heights of delicious sensation. This time, I completely lost consciousness when I went over my peak.

I was aware of only a few things during that time. Alex pressing gentle kisses to the miniscule wounds in

43

my neck. Alex cleaning both of us with a towel that he had retrieved from my dresser. Alex carefully covering me with the sheets and quilt. Pressing a heart-wrenching kiss against my damp forehead, donning his shorts again, closing the window. And as he left, stopping at my bedroom door and whispering with a world of emotion in his compelling tone.

"You didn't have to make me love you. I already did."

CHAPTER 4

The next morning, before I even opened my eyes, I knew I had been altered. Recalling the poignant events of the night before, I curled myself into a fetal position under the warmth of my sheet and heavy quilt, wincing at the unusual aches and pain as I moved.

What had I done? He'd come here and before he could voice his hate for me or act on it as he had the right to do, I'd thrown myself at him like some bar-fly whore. Groaning, I glanced over at the bright red numbers on my nightstand alarm clock. It was already eleven a.m.

What had he said as he was leaving? It seemed imminently important. A crucial little whisper of words that meant something serious, but I could not grasp them in my sleepy head. So many things needed to be done. Feed Sadie, my recently neglected Golden Retriever, feed Whiskers, my arrogant black cat who thought she owned the world. I would bet money her litter box desperately needed cleaning as well. Then the horses. Muck out the stalls, throw down hay from the loft, fill up water buckets, and ration out grain. Check on the whereabouts of Messenger.

Dragging myself out of bed was an exercise in torture. And while the rest of my body protested, I was surprised to see that my ankle looked and felt much better. The swelling had almost completely disappeared. I gingerly put both feet on the floor and tested my weight on the bad ankle. There was still a little tenderness, but at least I would not have to use the crutches.

Then I looked up and saw my reflection in the mirror over my dresser. Bruises, strikingly dark against the pallid tone of my skin, were peppered along my arms and shoulders. Fingerprints of the undead. I drew my hair away from the left side of my neck. There were no bite marks. A vision of Alex's face, as I remembered it from the night before, swam in my head. The desperation. The sorrow. Then I recalled my inevitable downfall. I had cast off my fear and anger and reached out to him with everything I could think to offer. He had taken it all and given in return. Confusion flooded me, as dark and glossy as the silk scarf lying across my dresser. I touched the scarf and then pulled it through my fingers slowly.

Alex. A little smile began to pull the corners of my mouth up. I may have felt battered on the outside, but inside I felt... happy. Content. Instinct made me want to question it, turn it over and look for the crack, read the manufacturer's warranty. I shook my head, tossed the scarf back down on the dresser, and looked at myself again.

A tremulous smile was there in the mirror. My eyes were shining. *Luminous*.

While I stood under the often-unreliable showerhead in my little bathroom and let the warm water trail down over the bruises, I tried not to think about it too much. I went over the chores I had to do, thought about a shopping list, whether I should repaint my bedroom. Simple things. By the time I was done with my shower, I felt energized and ready to face the day.

When I came downstairs and stepped into the kitchen, I came to an immediate halt.

The coffee was made. Whiskers was lapping at her water bowl, which had been filled. Her food dish was half-full of food. Sadie pranced in from the den, her tail waving madly. I sank my fingers into the soft golden fur around her neck and scratched.

"Sorry I've been so busy, sweetie." I gave her a quick hug and went to check her food bowl and Whiskers' litter box. The bowl was full of kibble and the litter box was clean. Coming back into the kitchen, I heard Nelly's familiar voice calling out.

"Good morning, honey." She walked in from the den smiling, but when she got a good look at me, she lost the smile and shrieked.

"Sarah! What in the world happened to you?" Her gaping eyes darted over me as she held out one of my bruised arms, "Who did this to you?"

I could not look her in the eye. How could I possibly explain what had happened between Alex and I? There was no way to say it delicately, and I knew she would not relent until she knew. I took a deep breath.

"Alex."

Her eyes grew wide and the expression on her face was one of stunned horror, "Oh, Sarah. No. How? Alex really did this?"

"He wasn't trying to hurt me. It was... consensual." It sounded so lame. And it did not come close to describing anything that had occurred. Only that he had not forced me. I shook my head and went to grab a coffee cup, "I know it looks bad, but it wasn't his fault. Honestly."

"He hurt you."

I poured the coffee, still lacking the courage to meet her stare, "Something happened while you were gone. There was a problem with the new vampires. You were right about them."

She moved to my side and gently grasped one arm, "But what about Alex? What happened to him?"

Finally, I raised my eyes to her face, "He was attacked, Nelly. It was horrible."

I explained everything to her as best as I could. Keeping a grip on my emotions while I talked about the battle and Alex was a monumental task, and several times I felt like I was about to bust out into tears. She listened to me patiently, rubbing my arm softly when I described how Michael insisted that it was my decision whether to save him.

"Oh, sweetie." She wrapped her arms around me and gripped me tightly for a few moments before pulling back and searching my face again, "Don't you blame yourself for this, you hear? It's natural to want to keep those you love close to you. Even if it means they have to change in order to stay."

"He told me he hated it when he was a vampire."

A sad little smile curved her lips, "Maybe he hated it because he felt alone. He has us now, doesn't he?"

I stared pensively at my coffee cup, contemplating what she said. She could be absolutely right. He didn't have to live the same kind of life he had before. Things could be different for him now. However, would my mother want to take him back with her to California? After what had happened the night before, I could not imagine him leaving.

"There's something else you should know." I said slowly, "My mother is back."

Her face lost all hint of color. She went to the kitchen table and sat down, her head bent. Words of comfort might have been appropriate, but I could not think of anything that might reassure her. If I had enough courage, I could go out to the meadow and demand answers. I could look Selena in the face and ask the question that had been burning through me ever since I found out she was still alive. *How could she leave her children?*

But I was a coward. I was afraid that the answer would hurt so much more than the question itself. What if there really was something so wrong with me that even my own mother could not put up with me? It was childish to jump to such a conclusion. However, the idea stuck and I had been carrying it around with me for weeks.

"I'm going out to feed the horses and clean stalls." I mumbled, grabbing my jacket from the peg by the back door. I did not want to see Nelly's face. I did not want to see pity there in her eyes, reflecting back at me like a beacon.

Thirty minutes later, I was sitting in a rusty old lawn chair at the end of the barn aisle and sobbing with my face in my hands. Whether my mother was in Indiana or in California, the damage had been done. I felt like I did not know who I was anymore. Warm tears seeped through my fingers and ran down my hands and arms.

Had my father honestly thought that I could handle all of this? Where would he get that impression? I remembered the letter that he had written and put inside the journal that had been passed down to me from my grandfather. He had wanted me to keep the vampire thing a secret from Katie, so that had to mean something.

Though I still struggled inside, I jerked myself to my feet and wiped the tears from my cheeks. I could not let it break me. I just couldn't. Dad had left me with something wonderful to take care of that had always been a part of my life. The inn was not perfect. There were repairs that needed to be made. Renovations could be done to modernize the bathrooms, if I could find the money somehow to make it happen. Changes could be made to it that would make it an even greater experience for those guests who chose to stay with us. And I was needed personally to keep it running.

Unfortunately, I was also the only one who could keep the inn itself separate from the vampires that walked around the place at night. I could not let them ruin what we had going on here. Keeping a leash on Michael and the others was *my* job. Nobody else's.

Raising my head to walk out of the barn, I decided I was not going to let anything prevent me from doing what I was meant to do. Not my mother. Not the vampires. Not the Council. This was mine.

Later, I made some calls to get some quotes on updating the bathrooms in the main house. I thoroughly cleaned the bedrooms upstairs with Nelly's help. She put together a beef stew in the slow cooker for our dinner, which left the house with the mouth-watering aroma of simmering beef, onions and the secret recipe of spices she used for her famous stew.

She did not ask me anything more about Alex, and we did not talk about my mother. When the shadows began to grow longer, and the last rays of the sun sent slanting golden rays down upon the yellowing grass of the front yard, I decided to meet Michael on his own turf before he could approach the house.

I told Nelly I would be back as soon as I could and asked her not to leave the house. Then I wrapped myself in a thick red wool cardigan and walked down the darkening lane heading for the meadow and the creek.

He would know in an instant that Alex and I had been together, if he was not already aware of it. However, I was not going to apologize for it. The soles of my beloved hiking boots tread silently through the night, leaving dark grooved prints in the evening dew and mud along the lane. When I reached the edge of the meadow, I looked around.

The creek was running a little slower than usual, its banks dotted here and there with gold and scarlet leaves, dry twigs laying like the bones of the damned upon the banks. The leaves of the big oak tree near the creek had begun to change colors. There were sparrows and robins calling brightly to each other in its high branches.

The grass in the meadow was trampled, bent, and battered by the footsteps of the undead who resided beneath it. I looked at it, sadness seeping in through the determination I had forged during my walk out there. I wished I could erase vampires from the face of the earth. Then, I remembered Alex.

A low growl emanated around me, seeming to come at me from all sides. It was followed by an urgent female's voice.

"Michael, no. Don't do this."

Then I saw three vampires standing across the clearing, their silhouettes rigid with tension in the early evening light. One of them turned to me, and I recognized the fierce face of Michael. Beside him, with one hand on his arm, stood Victoria. Three paces away stood my mother, looking annoyed.

Michael's voice swept towards me like a dark wave, the timbre of it rolling with fury.

"You let him bite you."

CHAPTER 5

An involuntary shiver snaked through my body at his tone. I took a deep breath and closed the distance between us. I did not belong to him, I reminded myself. Alex had come to me and I had given myself freely. Surprisingly, I still felt no regret about it. I also wondered where Alex might be and if he might show up to give me a little support. However, I could not wait on him.

"Michael, I know you're upset." I began, my eyes skipping over the other two vampires approaching us.

He came to stand directly in front of me, only a foot or so away. I could see the fury burning there, and my confidence began to ebb away.

"You let him bite you." Michael growled.

"He asked. I didn't deny him."

Victoria moved to put her hand on his shoulder, but he jerked away with a low, rumbling laugh, "Well, then. How was it? Everything you imagined?"

Pressing my lips together tightly, I glared at him and said nothing. Victoria approached me, her long evergreen cape trailing behind her. Her serious hazel eyes were hooded beneath thick amber eyelashes and her brows were drawn together in a look of concern. I kept my eyes locked on her. Victoria was one of the few vampires I felt I could trust, and I knew she understood me. I had suspected since we had first met that she was capable of reading my mind. In subtle ways, the first night we stood face to face, she had given me reasons to suspect she was sympathetic to my position.

"Michael, please be calm." She said tightly, glancing at him over her shoulder.

"Yes, please do show a bit of self control." My mother had moved closer to the three of us and stood near Michael, one hand on a hip in an insolent pose. She returned my hostile stare with a complacent tiny grin.

"You! This is your fault! It was you who sent him here!" Michael suddenly launched himself at my mother, fury written into his every feature. Before I could draw a breath, he had her down on the ground with his hands around her neck.

"You knew this would happen, didn't you?" He demanded, squeezing ever tighter against her throat. I watched, fascinated, as she struggled under him. He could not really kill her that way, could he? If he could, did I want that?

"Stop!" I shouted, jumping towards them and grabbing Michael's shoulder, "It's not her fault! No one made me do anything! I had sex with Alex because I wanted to."

Everything stopped. The hands gripping my mother's neck so forcefully slowly came away. Selena scrambled away from him, a devious smile on her smug face. Beneath my hand, Michael's broad shoulder stiffened. The anger radiating out from him touched me before he even turned his eyes on me. When I realized what I had done, I stumbled back from him as my mother had. Minus the smile.

"You *did what*?"

Oh, God. I should have kept my mouth shut. He threw back his head and roared. The sound was unlike anything I'd ever heard. The leaves on the trees trembled with the force of it. I slapped my hands over my ears, trying to mute the haunting sound of his rage.

Everything around me seemed to shimmer slightly, blurring and shuddering.

Hands grabbed for me, rough on the bruises beneath my cardigan. I winced and took a quick look to see who was manhandling me. Alex's concerned eyes met mine. When I looked over at Michael, I realized that both Victoria and Selena were physically holding him back from Alex and me. His fangs were bared, glittering like diamonds in the night. Alex's fingers tightened on my arms, pulling at me and then pushing me away from the meadow. Panic sliced through me, because I knew they could not hold him. No one could hold him.

Nelly was standing by my truck as we hurried back to the house. She apparently had started the truck and stood waiting with my faded leather wallet in her hand. Tossing the wallet into the truck, she gestured at both of us to hurry. I dove into the passenger seat, landing on the little black toolbox I usually carried around with me in the truck.

Alex wrenched the gearshift into drive, and the gravel under the tires flew up behind us as we made a U-turn in front of the house and went flying down the

driveway. I kept turning around, expecting to see
Michael rushing at us. My heart was pounding wildly,
and each breath felt like it might be my last. When we
came over the hill, I saw the gate was closed below us.

"Shit!" I turned to Alex, but before I could say
anything else, he put his foot on the brake and stared
straight ahead, his golden face dark with
determination. I turned to see what had stopped him
and choked back a sob.

Michael was in front of the gate, standing there
with clenched fists and his head lowered. His anger
was a physical force of its own, due to the fear he
induced. Looking at him as he stood down there
blocking our way out, I felt helpless. I had to get Alex
out of there. Michael would destroy him. I was
certain of it.

"He doesn't realize." Alex murmured softly. The
terror that had dominated him only a moment ago had
evaporated. He was entirely calm. I could only stare
at him. I briefly considered the idea that this beautiful
blond vampire sitting so still beside me could be
losing his mind. When he reached over and gripped

one of my hands, I felt a wave of uneasiness sweep over me.

He bowed his dazzling face down close to mine, his eyes clear and full of some dark, unknown purpose.

"Listen to me. I've got this." He trailed two fingers over the line of my jaw, leaving a trail of chills that spread from my face into my neck and down the curve of my spine. God, I did not want to lose him. What did he think he was doing? Michael was centuries older than he was.

"No, no. Alex, you can't fight him. You don't know his power." I gasped.

He gave me a level look with narrowed green eyes, and I watched a forbidding half smile curl up one side of his mouth. It was devious and something wholly unexpected. When he spoke again, his words were low and ripe with violence.

"He doesn't know mine."

"But…" He opened the door and got out. I saw him start striding down the hill towards Michael at the end of the driveway, "Shit!" I sputtered and pushed the passenger-side door open. I could not think straight. Shouldn't I have anticipated this moment? I should have had a plan. However, no solution presented itself as I stumbled along after Alex, grabbing at his arm and begging him to stop.

A flash of motion in the corner of my eye alerted me to the fact that we were not alone. Victoria and Selena were standing by the truck; both of them looking like Michael had given them quite a fight. Victoria's hair had fallen almost completely out of its elegant chignon and was blowing loosely around her in tawny tangles. My mother was holding her right arm at a strange angle, and her outfit was splattered with dirt and blood. I assumed it was her own, but I saw no open wounds.

Alex glanced coldly over his shoulder at the other two vampires, "Stay out of this. I'm not going to keep running from him. It ends here."

A dark chuckle came at us from Michael. His eyes were entirely black under those exquisitely arched eyebrows. Every ounce of power he was holding back had gathered there in the fathomless depths of those eyes, and they were taking in the scene with hard calculation.

"On a suicide mission, Golden Boy?" Michael said.

"Alex, please. Don't try to fight him." I begged, casting furtive glances over my shoulder at Victoria. *Do something*, I shouted at her in my head. *For God's sake, Michael's really going to kill him*!

Victoria shook her head and then her gaze swiveled back towards Michael.

"I'll only warn you once, Michael." Alex advised in a shallow hiss of sound, "Things are different now. My powers have evolved far beyond what you might think."

His dark opponent laughed, and he lowered himself into a predatory crouch. There was an explosion of sound, like a hard breeze whistling through a narrow doorway. Then a flash of yellow light, so bright in the center it hurt my eyes. I felt a massive shift in the energy around me—some odd vibration that penetrated the layers of my skin and struck me numb for a moment. I could not tell what happened. I only knew that Michael had moved to attack.

When I was finally able to see again, it was only in dull outlines. I rubbed at my eyes, hoping desperately that it was only temporary. The sounds around me were rough and indistinct, but I recognized the light timbre of Victoria's voice.

"Michael, talk to me. Can you hear me?" She said.

There was a low, mumbled reply. Then I felt Alex's familiar arms around me, holding my trembling body. I needed something to keep me together in one piece. It was dreadful not knowing what was happening, imagining the worst, and dreading the images that might eventually penetrate into the fog I was living in.

I reached up and grasped Alex's face in my hands. "I can't see."

"You'll be fine in a few minutes."

A weary groan rose up a few feet in front of me. Michael.

"What happened?" I demanded, turning from Alex and trying to refocus my vision and my thoughts.

"Sit down for a few minutes until your sight clears." With gentle hands, he lowered me so that I was kneeling on the grass. The moist earth beneath me felt real and thoroughly familiar. I drew a few desperate breaths and blinked.

Finally, things were beginning to shift into recognizable forms. One vampire on the ground. Another slender vampire kneeling by the fallen. And when I looked up, an enchanting angel standing over me, his green eyes clear and sure. I tore my gaze away from Alex's face with great difficulty and looked over at Michael.

He was lying on his side, curled up and holding his head in both hands. The ebony strands of his hair were spilling through the gaps between his fingers. He was in agony. He moaned again, a plaintive sound that pierced through the fear he had induced in me only a few moments ago. As the landscape around us became completely clear to me once more, I shuddered.

The urge to try to help Michael was overwhelming, and I crawled forward, casting a quick look at Victoria, who was patiently waiting by his side. Alex hissed a warning at me and moved to intercept my progress, but I glared at him over my shoulder.

"Don't, Alex. Give me a minute."

I did not wait for his reaction. When I reached Michael, I laid one cold hand against his shoulder. He was shaking like a frightened child. Michael just did not do that. I looked up at Victoria in terror, "What happened?"

"He tried to attack Alex." She searched for more words, but ended up just shaking her head. She lowered herself closer to him, like a gray dove settling next to her lifelong mate on a bare winter branch. Hesitation gripped me suddenly as I watched her. What was this between them? Some cruel, dark emotion rose inside me, blackening that rosy image I had conjured of Michael and me moving side-by-side in broad daylight. Like a couple.

I had lost something. But what had been there before I destroyed it? Lust? A blooming love, uncertain and shy? No. Something beyond my own comprehension. It was gone then. If I were to try to fight for this elusive lost treasure, would those witnesses turn away to offer some measure of privacy or respect? No. So I determined that it would have to wait. For some other cold place and time.

Slipping a frosty lid over my fragile emotional state, I rose slowly to my feet. I noticed the stray hairs that swept away from Victoria's cheek and settled on the fabric of Michael's dark cotton shirt. Like they belonged there.

"Alex, please help Victoria get Michael back into the caves." The sound of my voice was bleak. I did not turn to confirm that Alex had heard me. I trudged back to my truck, got behind the wheel, and drove down to the gate. Still closed. Sighing, I started to get out.

Then I saw my mother. She moved very quickly, unhooked the chain from around the post, and swung the gate open without even turning towards me. I didn't want to see the look on her face anyway. I did not want her to see me, lost and frustrated.

CHAPTER 6

The trees, fences, mailboxes, and driveways along the road were silent observers to my flight from home. Silent and condemning, it seemed to me. No matter where I looked, I found no solace. Not in the sleepy dark homes that I passed. Not in the music on my old radio. Clapton was singing about how his beautiful blond had been so wonderful. Well, good for her.

As I got closer to town, I saw the neon half-lit sign for Bill's Bar glowing cheaply in the ebony air of the evening. Perfect. Slowing down, I surveyed the parking lot cautiously. Trevor's uniquely pimped out black Dodge Ram was not parked in the small gravel lot by the building, so I decided to take a chance. I also saw the dusty hatchback that belonged to my best friend from high school, Kara.

When you go to high school in a small town, you get used to just about everyone you know leaving for college after graduation and not moving back. Nashville is a small town, unlike its namesake in Tennessee. There are not very many jobs to be had around here. All the high-school kids catch the part-time work in the restaurants and gift shops. A few college graduates might get a position managing one of the larger inns, but for the most part, there is nothing here for college graduates. Therefore, the majority of my friends from high school moved away. Except for Kara.

Kara Beauchamp originally moved into town with her parents and her big brother Matt back in 2002. Their parents were determined to open their own boutique for dogs, selling ridiculous-looking little capes and boots to the upper-class families that make it a point to come down to Brown County several times a year. They called the place Sassy Bitches, a name that raised a huge storm of controversy within the social circles of our little town. Despite the local uproar over the name of the store, the Beauchamps hung on resolutely, and during an off-season slump in sales, Kara's mom, Carol set up a website and began to sell their products online. It became an overnight success and drew a lot of attention to their tiny little store off Main Street. Kara became an integral part of the business structure, because she knew so much about online marketing. She had decided to stick around Brown County once things really took off. This was great for both of us.

However, when I found out that my Dad was sick and everyone around me was dripping with concern and pity, I began to shut people out of my life. That included Kara. By the time Dad passed away, she and I only spoke when we ran into each other by chance at the grocery store. Those had been awkward, hasty conversations that always made me feel like a complete shit for slamming the door so suddenly on our friendship.

As I sat in the parking lot of Bill's, I considered not going inside. This was just another relationship that was messed up in my insignificant little world. I was not really in the mood to try to fix anything. However, for some reason, I pushed away the doubts and fear. I found a parking space around the corner from the main entrance, pulled in slowly and put the truck in park.

Grabbing my wallet, I stepped out of the truck into the chilly night air and took a deep steadying breath. It was going to be okay. I'll just have a drink or two and then go home. No problem, I thought.

When I opened the heavy wood door, a rush of noise and cigarette smoke assaulted me. Somebody was playing Metallica on the jukebox that glowed in the corner between groups of talking people. There were small explosions of laughter here and there. One of the waitresses was serving pitchers of beer to a group of guys by the pool table.

I looked to the bar where the owner, Bill Gibson, was deep in conversation with the high-school football coach. Bill's grim expression and the shaking of his head indicated that Coach Morton had probably just been cut off from the Jack and Cokes he reportedly had too many of each night.

There were a few empty bar stools. I chose one closest to the door in case I needed to make a socially unacceptable hasty exit. I had not seen Kara yet, but I had only gone over the crowd for a second to make sure that Trevor was not there. It was always possible that one of his friends might have driven him to the bar. Or one of the dozen or so clueless women who imagined that he was telling the truth when he said he loved them.

"You're not twenty one yet." Bill teased gently, snapping me back from my bitter musings. He came over to me with a towel draped across one shoulder. My Dad had been friends with Bill since they had been in grade school together. Both of them had grown up here. A year after my Mom left us, Bill's amazingly sweet wife, Kathy, had died from breast cancer. It was the kind of loss that draws old friends together in hard times.

"According to my birth certificate, I'm twenty three," I replied with a faint smile, "But a lot of times I feel like a forty year old."

He grinned and shook his head, "You have no idea, kid."

"How have you been?" I asked.

He shrugged and pulled a couple beer mugs from the shelf over his head, "Up and down. Waiting for the fall rush, like everybody else. What do you want to drink, Sarah?"

"I'm thinking it's a night for hurricanes."

Bill's dark eyebrows rose, "You sure about that?"

I thought about everything that had happened in the last few weeks. The pain, the confusion, the on-going crush of anger. I nodded with a sigh and slid my credit card across the smooth surface of the bar, "Start me a tab, Bill."

Halfway through the first Hurricane, I felt my arms and legs go heavy with the amount of alcohol beginning to flow through my bloodstream. Having not made a habit of ingesting alcohol on a regular basis, it hit me rather quickly. By the time I finished the second one, Bill had confiscated my keys, and the guy sitting next to me had begun to chat me up. Unfortunately, he was pretty disgusting and three times as drunk as I was.

"Sarah?"

I turned a little too fast on the barstool and almost took a nosedive into the lap of the guy next to me. Instead, I ended up half off the stool and hanging precariously onto the edge of the bar. Kara was standing behind me with a familiar smirk on her face.

"Hi Kara!" I lurched forward and grabbed her up in a big bear hug, "It's so good to see you!"

"Gee, are we a little drunk tonight?" She wiggled her carefully plucked red eyebrows at Bill, who shrugged and chuckled.

74

"I am *not* drunk."

"Bill, did you take this girl's keys yet?"

He held them up with a pinky finger, "You going to drive her home?"

Kara regarded me doubtfully as I grinned at her. She was my best friend. I just loved Kara. A couple times during our senior year, we skipped our last class of the day and went to the park by the school to trade sips from her Dad's flask of Bacardi while we talked about her latest boyfriend. Those were the days.

"I've missed you so much." I noticed with a vague sense of hilarity that my words kept coming out slurred. I giggled at myself and grabbed Kara by the arm, "Let's play pool!"

"Well, look what the cat dragged in."

I turned my head to the tall guy who had spoken. My mood plummeted almost immediately. Son of a bitch.

Kara rolled her eyes, "Oh, shit. Here we go."

Trevor Kincaid was eyeing me with a mix of pleasure and derision. Rob and Dave Miller were apparently his wingmen for the evening. The Miller brothers were notorious party boys even though Rob was technically married with three kids. That did not exactly stop him from flirting, but it should have kept him from picking up younger women on the side when his wife of twelve years was sitting at home, miserable and tired after a long day working as a sixth-grade teacher. I had always felt a particular revulsion to Rob ever since he had made up a rumor about me performing a sexual maneuver on him when we were still in high school. He was essentially a pathological liar. Therefore, he and Trevor were perfect BFF's.

Stepping up to Trevor, I poked him hard in the chest with my index finger, "You picked the wrong night to come to this bar, asshole." I hiccupped loudly.

"Sarah, don't go there." Kara whispered.

"Oh, I *want* to go there. This guy here, he's a complete fucking loser."

Trevor chuckled and gripped my hand to stop my poking, "Chill out, Sarah. No need to stir up trouble."

"Damn, bitch. Just let it go." Rob said.

"And *you*." I wrenched myself away from Trevor, loser-asshole-of-the-world, to take on Rob, cheating-lying-piece-of-crap-with-a-bald-head dude, "Where's your wife tonight, Rob? Sitting home alone *again* while you pick up sluts to bang in your truck? Tell me this. When Tracey finally gets her head out of her ass, takes the kids, and leaves your sorry ass, where do you think you'll be? Alone in a bare apartment with nobody to talk to except the anonymous bitches you hit up on the internet."

"You stupid little country fuck…" He countered.

"Brilliant comeback, Rob." I giggled. Yes, he was a *genius*.

"We're leaving now." Kara announced, dragging me to the front door. I wanted to stay and finish my Hurricane. I wanted to kick Rob in the balls and smack Trevor. However, when the chilly night air struck me, I wobbled weakly and leaned against the brick wall near the door. It was so cold out there. In addition, my stupid legs were not working right.

"Are you going to throw up?"

I shook my head, which made me giggle, because everything looked strange when I moved like that. I heard Kara sigh in frustration and then the jingle of her keys, "Look, I'm parked three blocks down by the shop. *Do not* go anywhere." She held my chin in her hand for a second, "Sarah? You heard me, right? Don't go back in the bar. I'll be right back to pick you up."

"Oh, sure."

When I heard her heels clicking away into the distance, I looked around and noticed things seemed unusually quiet. I staggered across the sidewalk towards the curb and belched. That was when the door opened behind me, and the silence in the street was destroyed by the laughter, music, and pandemonium that echoed from the bar.

"I think we need to talk."

Great, I thought. Trevor again. Another belch tried to make its way up from my stomach.

"You shouldn't be talking to me at all." I said, trying to sound serious.

Things changed. Trevor's face, the energy around me, the air itself. He reached out and grabbed me around the waist, yanking me away from the front of the bar and into the alley that ran back towards the parking lot. I fought him. I scratched, kicked, and even ripped the pocket on his designer-label shirt when I tried to twist away from him.

"Let me go, you asshole!"

He shoved me up against a brick wall and pressed his forearm against my throat. I felt like I was going to be sick. His eyes were chilling, swirling with rage, and fear rushed over me in a black cloud. He was serious. And he wanted to hurt me.

CHAPTER 7

"I'm getting so sick of you, you cocky little bitch."
He growled, slamming a knee into my left side. I
dropped like a rock, gasping and sputtering with pain.
It was suddenly hard to draw a breath, and each one
blazed through me like a torch. I curled up onto my
side on the dirty pavement and desperately tried to
keep from screaming.

Trevor kneeled down and grasped a handful of my
hair, "I'm not taking any more of your shit, Sarah.
Are we clear on that?"

I blinked. During the little instant while my eyelids
were closed, something else had happened. When I
opened my eyes, I saw that a hand gripped Trevor's
arm, and Alex's familiar form stood poised beside my
attacker. His eyes were blazing with rage.

"You need to let go of her hair right now." His
voice was hard and cold, but a challenging little smile
was on his face.

Trevor turned his head to look at Alex, "Mind your
own business, dick."

Then I saw Alex's other hand curl around Trevor's wrist and squeeze. Trevor's brown eyes went wide with shock and pain, and he let go of my hair. However, Alex did not let go. I saw his features brighten with a bizarre and menacing expression. Then I heard a loud crack, and Trevor roared in anguish, staring down at his arm in abject horror.

Below his elbow, the arm had been broken in half. His hand dangled, lifeless and useless. Above, a sharp rod of white bone had jabbed through the skin. Blood dripped slowly onto the pavement in the alley as Trevor's screaming escalated.

"Oh, my God!"

Alex swept me away from the scene. The cold air rushed through my hair and over my chilled skin. Before I even had time to react, we were inside my truck and Alex was behind the wheel. He kept glancing in the rearview mirror as I stared at him. He began driving so fast that I had to hang onto the dashboard to keep from flying around the inside of the cab.

"Alex, slow down! We have to call an ambulance. Why did you do that?" I screeched at him.

"Just hush for a second. I have to think." He replied, flying up the dark road towards the inn.

The gate was open, and the rear end of the truck slid sideways in the gravel as we came onto the property. I suddenly realized that Michael had been right. Alex did not need permission to enter or leave the containment area. He had no limits. It was a frightening thought, especially after seeing the damage he had done to Trevor's arm in my defense.

He slammed on the brakes in front of the house. I stared ahead through the grungy windshield, suddenly feeling numb and strangely unattached to everything around me. I kept seeing the way Trevor's broken bone had poked through flesh of his arm. The blood. Oh, God.

The passenger door jerked open. Alex grabbed me by the arm and began dragging me effortlessly toward the front door.

"Stop it! Let me go!"

He did not do as I asked until we were past the front door. Nelly came rushing in from the kitchen, wringing her hands, "What happened?"

I jerked away from Alex, "I can't believe you did that. His fucking arm is *broken*, Alex!"

"Language!" Nelly hissed.

Alex turned simmering green eyes towards her, "Some jerk was attacking her. I had to do something."

"Who?"

"It was Trevor." I tore myself out of my cardigan and stalked into the kitchen. Everything was happening too fast for me. First the confrontation with Michael, then the fight between him and Alex, then the bar incident. I flopped down into a chair at the kitchen table and stared at the wall.

The chair next to me was moved back, and Alex sat down next to me. I heard him sigh before he started talking. I did not really want to hear what he had to say, though. The violence of the events I had witnessed over the course of the evening had left me exhausted and sad.

"Sarah, I'm sorry if I went overboard with that guy. But he was going to hurt you."

I crossed my arms on the tabletop and dropped my head, preferring not to respond.

"I can't let anything happen to you. Don't you understand?"

Turning my head finally, I watched him through the locks of my hair draped over my arm. It was so hard to digest the fact that such an angelic-looking creature could do so much damage. I studied the curve of his jaw, the tiny little cleft in his chin, the way his thick brown eyelashes drew the gaze towards his amazing eyes. I loved the fact that his mouth was just soft enough to kiss, but still looked so masculine.

But I hated what he was capable of doing.

"I need you to go away for a little while, Alex."

His eyebrows drew together in confusion, "But Sarah, I can't leave you by yourself."

Holding up one hand, I shook my head, "A few days. That's all. I just need a little time."

"You have visitors, Sarah." Nelly called from the entryway.

I shot a curious look at Alex and got up. It could not be Michael. When I made it to the front hall, Nelly was standing by the door with an odd look on her face, as if she had seen something she could not quite process.

"Who is it?" I asked her.

When she did not answer, I pulled the door open all the way. Victoria and my mother were standing on the porch. They had cleaned themselves up since the fight, but the expressions on their faces were forbidding. Great. It seemed like the longest night of my life. I took a deep breath and turned to Nelly.

"Just go up to bed. I'll lock everything up."

A tinge of anger sparked in her blue eyes, but she kept her head and went upstairs without another word to anyone. I certainly was not expecting it to be that easy. Turning back to my guests, I stepped out onto the porch. Alex had followed me, and he closed the door behind us then took up an uneasy stance beside me.

Victoria nodded briskly at both of us, "I'm glad you're both here. Michael needs blood."

I felt Alex's warm fingers tangle with mine, and I did not pull my hand away. Victoria noticed the move with a darting glance down at our hands and then sighed, "I am going to Indianapolis to meet with a contact that can provide him with bagged blood until he fully recovers."

"How badly is he hurt?" I asked.

"He'll be fine. As long as he doesn't try to attack Alex again."

He shifted beside me, "I had to defend myself."

Victoria held up her hand, "I don't think you understand the power inside you. Whatever happened out there, you will need to control it if you're going to help Sarah."

I groaned inwardly when I remembered what he had done to Trevor. It was very unlikely that asshole was going to keep his mouth shut about the unnaturally powerful guy who had broken his arm. Trevor's father was an attorney at a lucrative firm in Bloomington. The whole thing was going to become very complicated. Another *huge* complication.

"I need your permission to go." Victoria said.

Nodding, I pulled my hand from Alex and wrapped my arms around myself, "You have my permission to leave the containment field."

She reached out with a white card in her hand, and looked at me somberly, "My cell phone number. Call me if you need anything. I should be back in a day or two."

I pushed the card into one of the back pockets of my jeans. When she turned to go, my mother did not follow her. She stood there and watched me with a frown creasing her mouth. Alex touched my arm, and I knew what he was asking before he even said a word.

"Yes, I'll talk to her alone." I murmured.

He disappeared into the shadows of the yard like a ghost, barely touching the ground. I listened for the sound of leaves under his feet, but heard only the dull thud of my own heart. What could I say to this woman? Did it matter if she offered any excuses or apologies?

"I'm leaving too." She began smoothly, "Alex is well equipped to deal with any problems that might develop. I understand that you two have become... closer?"

I sighed and studied the dark shapes of the trees against the horizon, "Things have changed. He may be in some danger after tonight."

She laughed, "I don't think so. By giving him your blood, you've given him true immortality."

"What?"

Her lips arched in a mocking smile, "The Breath-Giver gave him his humanity back, but she also gave him something else. When Michael and Victoria drained him completely, what they didn't know was that he couldn't be killed. He didn't need to be resurrected."

"So he's what? A god?" This further bit of information was alarming.

"He's a Guardian." Irritated at my lack of understanding, she rolled her eyes, "Look, the Breath-Giver is a Seraph. An angel, fairy, or whatever. She chose Alex for you. When Michael turned him, she was furious. She was the one who influenced the Council to punish him. What she didn't count on was him being sent here."

"Holy crap." Michael was locked up because he had turned Alex. No wonder there was such animosity between them.

"Exactly. Therefore, when Alex was hurt, it was not serious. He would have recovered. But they gave him their blood. Then he had your blood as well." She sighed and turned her gaze on the dark trees before us, "Now what you've got is a Guardian angel vampire who can never be killed or repelled." She focused on me again and reaching forward, wrapped her fingers around my upper arms. Her eyes were hollow and dark as she stared at me, "If his temperament changes, if he becomes angry and difficult, no one can stop him. You'll need to keep him happy, Sarah."

Well, shit. She let go of me slowly and then moved away.

"I know you probably hate me. That's fine. I doubt that I can change that. But you need to know that I'm still looking out for you."

Heat had begun building inside my chest as she spoke. I had so many questions I wanted to ask her, so many insults I wanted to hurl at her. More than all that, I had to know why. Why did she give us up? How could it have come down to that? Bitter tears began to flow from my eyes, and I turned away to keep her from seeing them. No one should see me cry. Especially not her.

After a few minutes had passed and I heard nothing further, I looked and saw that I was alone once more. A cool breeze flowed against my face, blowing my hair back off my shoulders. I smelled leaves dying. I felt the earth beneath me go frigid. What I feared was that it was my own heart that was taking its last breath.

When I curled up in my bed later, it was almost dawn. My left side ached where Trevor had kneed me. My ankle was throbbing lightly. Alex had not returned, and I was relieved. I wished I could just leave everything behind and be alone. However, if I relinquished my role as Warden, it would fall on Katie.

When the yellow walls of my rooms began to grow brighter with the coming light, and my eyelids could barely open, a familiar manly figure slipped in through the door. He moved carefully and quietly, undressing in the pale light and sliding between the sheets of my bed. He wrapped a golden arm around my waist and sighed softly.

I was too exhausted to argue and far too comfortable to push him away. The warmth of his body lying nestled against me was a balm to my battered soul. I fell asleep in the arms of a god.

CHAPTER 8

"Sarah..."

Firm, urgent fingers stroked over the skin of my stomach and then lower, sending waves of pleasure to my head. Michael's face was so clear, so poignant and wracked with desire that my body responded blindly. A warm tongue lapped delicately at one of my nipples. I stretched, moaned, and slowly became aware that I was not dreaming.

The light coming in through the windows was limited by the clouds in the sky and painted dull shapes across the floor and walls, but it was obviously late in the morning. The golden locks of hair that brushed against my breast told me that my dream may have been about Michael, but it was Alex who was carefully and thoroughly stoking the desire rising within me.

"No biting." I whispered. I was not entirely sure what kind of power I had given him when he drank from me, but thought it would be better to hold off on that particular activity until I could find out more.

There was a moment of hesitation before he began again, pushing me closer and closer to the edge of ecstasy, then backing off and just stroking my arm lazily, his mesmerizing green eyes locked on my flushed face. When he rose from the bed, he stretched slowly and gave me an impish little wink before pushing his boxers down over his hips and knees.

Looking at him there, standing bare, strong, and beautiful before me, I again felt that peculiar compulsion to let him take anything he wanted. As if I belonged to him and it was all in his right to demand. When he lowered himself over me, every ounce of power he possessed and every gorgeous detail of his body sent me fully into that frame of mind. I forgot about everyone else. I forgot about the meadow. I dismissed the warnings of my mother and Victoria.

His movements inside me and his gentle murmurs against my ear sent me spiraling up into a world I had never known. When I came crashing back down to earth, he was feasting on my blood. All I could do was watch. He had drawn one of my thighs up over his shoulder and clamped his mouth down upon the femoral artery there, so close to where he had spilled his seed only moments before.

"Alex…" I whispered hoarsely, barely finding the energy to say his name, "No."

He did not even look over at me. His mouth and throat were working just fine, but apparently, he had gone deaf. I managed to lift my right arm, but I had no strength left in the muscles. All I managed to do was to move it over a few inches on the bed.

The door was suddenly thrown open and crashed against the wall. Finally, he looked up. That's when I saw the blood on him. Then I saw Nelly standing in the doorway, her blue eyes fierce and determined.

"You get away from her this instant, Alexander."

With bright red blood dripping from his mouth onto my ravaged thigh, he stared at her in astonishment. I looked down at myself and whimpered like a child. There was so much blood. It was still gushing out of me, over the sheet in an ever-widening circle.

"Out!" Nelly shouted at him.

"But she needs me to close it! She'll die!"

Nelly turned to him with a growl, "Get Michael to do it. *Now*."

I closed my eyes. A world of looming gray shadows was calling me, urging me to let go—to come into the darkness. I felt the presence of many lost souls, moaning in confusion and loss. I did not want to go there. There had to be another place. Somewhere bright and warm with laughter. Maybe my father would be there.

Later, Michael's voice moved over me. It was a guide, a compass pointing the way to somewhere I felt I belonged, "You've lost a lot of blood, but I've sealed the wounds. I am here. I won't let it happen again."

Everything was still gray around me, but there was warmth blooming from somewhere inside. Gentle hands holding me, Michael's deep calming voice urging me onward.

"Come back, love. You're all right now. Come back."

Nelly's voice interjected quietly, "Alex won't wait much longer."

The gentle voice beside me morphed into the snarl of a dangerous animal, "If he doesn't do as he's told,

I'm bringing Isaiah into this. Alex may be stronger than I am, but let him try to attack the oldest vampire on earth. Then we'll see exactly how much his power is worth."

Who was Isaiah? My eyelids still felt heavy, but I forced them open. There was daylight coming through the windows. It was not sunny outside. There were masses of high gray clouds filtering the sun. Turning my head, I looked wonderingly upon the face of my prisoner.

He looked exhausted. There was a gray cast to his skin that I had never seen before. He must have felt me move, because he turned his gaze on me expectantly, the blue eyes coming alive with hope. Then he slid his thick arms under my back and pressed me gently against him, gathering me in an embrace.

"Never again." I felt the rumble of his voice through his chest, "I nearly lost you."

"What are you thinking, Michael?" Nelly asked, suspicion peppering her tone.

He did not answer her. Drawing back from me a little, he closed his eyes and rested his forehead against mine. His skin was a little cool but firm. Then something strange began to happen.

In my head, I felt a pull. As if there was some force inside me reaching out for Michael and making everything it could from the contact. It was a whirling golden rope, tossed out to find its mate. In the place where our foreheads were touching, I felt a slow heat begin to burn. It was not uncomfortable at all. It was rather soothing.

Then he spoke to me. Without words.

Are you feeling this?

I wanted to move away.

Don't. Try to talk to me.

Taking a deep breath, I tried to concentrate on the vibrations he was sending through me. However, the dream I had about him that morning kept replaying itself in my head. That was the last thing I wanted him to see. Jerking back from him, I struggled to push his arms away.

"Let me go, Michael." He moved back, and I drew the patchwork quilt closer around me. As if that aged cotton could hold back a creature of immense power.

I looked over at Nelly, who kept watching Michael suspiciously.

"How are you here? It's daytime." I demanded.

A half smirk emerged on his face, and he waved a hand, "I'm a magician of the highest order. I never reveal my secrets."

Nelly snorted. Ignoring them both, I lifted up the covers and stared down at my thigh where Alex had bitten me. There was no indication that I had suffered any injury at all. Stunned, I looked back over at Michael.

"You fixed this?" I squeaked, "How?"

"Vampire venom," Nelly answered, handing me a cup of tea on a saucer, "It's pretty amazing stuff."

I gratefully accepted the tea, "Thanks, Nelly."

Michael patted my leg and stood as if preparing to leave. He staggered for a moment, grabbing the back of the chair he had been sitting in. I saw him close his eyes and press his long fingers against his temple.

"Sit back down," I said, "You can't go outside like that. Nelly, did Victoria get back with the blood yet?"

"No. She called a while ago and said she got held up."

"Damn it. We have to help him somehow." I cursed my weakened state, and eyed Michael warily as he lowered himself back into the armchair by my bed. Thinking quickly, I turned to Nelly, "Would you mind getting my cell phone? I think it's in the truck. Or maybe the barn."

Her head tilted slightly as she looked at me and then back at Michael. She gathered up some sheets from the floor by my closet, and I clearly saw that they were soaked with blood. It made my head spin, thinking about how close I had come to death.

When I heard Nelly descend the stairs, I reached out and grasped one of Michael's cold hands, "You need blood. If I could give you some of mine, I would."

He shook his head, "No. I could not do that."

"Then I give you permission to leave the containment field."

I saw his beautiful eyes begin to shine with hope, and the gray tone to his skin faded minutely. However, the light in his eyes diminished when my strength left me. My hand was limp between the two of his. I wanted to keep my eyes open. I wanted to give him more to hope for. I longed desperately to see that emotion flood his features.

"Go and find what you need. Then come back." I requested.

He sighed and pressed my fingers to his cool lips, "I can't believe you're letting me walk away. How do you know I'll come back?"

I considered the question seriously for a few seconds. I knew by the way his gaze caressed me. I knew because of the warmth in his words and the way he had held me. Michael would not leave me as long as I needed him. Taking a shallow breath, I smiled at him kindly and then closed my eyes.

CHAPTER 9 - MICHAEL

Freedom. It is such a little word. When men say the word, they know nothing about the true meaning. Perhaps if a man has been locked up for 65 years, he may comprehend the enormity of the concept. When I staggered down that quiet country road and met no invisible shield to hold me in, it was a rebirth.

For a fraction of a second, I recalled the sight of Sarah lying in that bed. Her helplessness, her tangled hair, the blood rushing forth. I tried not to remember that other girl, the one in New York, bleeding out on the pavement as Isaiah's guards descended on me. If they had not come, she would be alive, I assured myself. But perhaps not. I was not known for my mercy at that time. I also knew that resurrection of my past misdeeds was always destined to cause misery.

Instead of berating myself for past wrongs, I focused on my most pressing need.

Just when I spotted an elderly woman making her way towards her mailbox near the end of the road, a dark sedan came speeding up towards me. It came to a screeching halt next to me on the cold pavement. Victoria.

"Michael, get in." She had the window rolled down, and I could see the cooler in the backseat. There would be bags of cooled blood inside. I cast one yearning glance towards the warm-blooded human staring at us suspiciously from her dirt driveway. One human death in a town of this size would draw a great deal of unwanted attention.

Resigned, I climbed into the passenger seat beside Victoria. Before she took off, she reached behind her, shoved the lid of the cooler aside, and threw three full bags of blood into my lap. Without a word, I ripped the cap from the first one and sucked it down. It rolled down my throat like sweet syrup, the coppery taste infusing me with power that I felt in every cell of my body.

"You must have found Meekah." I mumbled.

She nodded, her eyes fixed on the road with precise concentration. "She's waiting for us in Chicago."

Meekah was one of my special projects from long ago. During one particularly hot summer I spent in Paris, I heard a rumor from another vampire about a young girl who could foresee the future. It was July of 1746. I'd been carousing drunkenly with a group of ambassadors from England for several months and was growing weary of them all, when I discovered, quite by accident, that there was a vampire posing a representative of Spain in Paris. One of the English fellows related to me an unremarkable story about how this pretender kept odd hours. When I pressed him for further information, he relayed to me that the Spanish ambassador was rumored to be a creature of the night and had drained two kitchen maids of their blood.

I was not pleased. It was ridiculously sloppy for a vampire to have exposed himself in such a way. With our speed and our ability to compel those around us to forget what they have seen, it has always been relatively easy to keep our true nature a carefully guarded secret from humankind. My place in Parisian society had been a role that I created with great care. I enjoyed my freedom, the opulence in which I lived day to day, and the knowledge that every drop of blood I took from a human would remain my own secret.

It was easy for me to find the culprit. Being a cautious creature, I did not immediately burst in upon him in his bed to demand explanations. For a week, I followed him from place to place. I watched him dine with royalty and talk earnestly with secretaries and clergymen. From dark corners, I witnessed the money that changed hands as he bribed his way into the highest society parties. The French would never trust a Spaniard, but they would accept his money in exchange for invitations to bright, glittering balls and fifteen-course dinner parties where only the very best food was served.

One night I watched him go into the back room of a dingy tavern by the docks, and I saw him recklessly murder a barmaid. He had bent her backwards over a rough wooden table cluttered with half-eaten plates of food. While he drained her, flies buzzed lazily throughout the room. Their incessant buzzing was enough to drive anyone mad.

The filth of the place combined with his thoughtless actions sickened me. Ending his pathetic existence was foremost in my mind. When he looked up from his latest victim to find me standing there in that disgusting place, he seemed genuinely surprised. Perhaps he had thought he was immune from the dark justice that other vampires often dealt out to their peers. Perhaps he believed that he was the only undead creature roaming the Paris streets for blood.

"What do you want?" He growled.

I attacked him without answering. It was rather messy. After I ripped off one of his legs, he began to beg. That sort of ploy did not typically have much effect on me. I was heartless when it came to disciplining my own kind.

When the tavern owner rushed in after hearing the ambassador's screams, I compelled him to turn around and act as if he'd seen nothing amiss. The putrid creature before me whimpered and moaned in his pain.

"Please spare me."

"Not possible."

"I have money!" He stammered.

"I am far richer."

His face tensed again in agony as I began pulling off one arm at the shoulder. Then he whispered so quietly that only a creature with superior hearing could understand.

"There is a girl I know who sees visions of the future."

I paused in my work, eyeing him with disbelief. I had been a vampire for more than a hundred years, and I had heard of only three individuals in the world who could accurately predict the future. Considering my growing lack of affection for Paris, the heat, the endless drunken nights in gloomy strange rooms, I was ripe for a new adventure.

"Where?" I demanded.

"I will show you. Please."

Although I still held an intense hatred for the creature and doubted his word, I agreed to mend him if he would lead me to the girl. It required a good deal of my venom, but I managed to heal him enough to be sure that he would have the ability to live up to his end of the bargain. I quickly disposed of the dead bar maid and took him to my townhouse on Saint Germain. He insisted on accompanying me to where the seer lived, explaining that I would never be able to find it on my own. Naturally, I did not trust him. I am no fool.

When I took the poker from the fireplace and shoved it through his chest, right near his heart, he finally complied with my request.

"She's a seamstress for a theater in London. Drury Lane." He gasped.

"What's her name?"

"Meekah." A trickle of blood appeared at the corner of his mouth, "She's African."

I tore his head off.

Several weeks later, I met her for the first time. She barely spoke English at all, but appeared to be very intelligent. She told me that she had seen me coming. She had known where we would meet. She also knew that I was going to turn her into a vampire. Without resistance, she accepted the attention and gifts that I lavished on her.

We spent the fall in a remote village near Bath. She had two servants, a little white dog, and garden. The cottage was not very large, but it was adequate for our needs. All I wanted was for her to be comfortable and to begin to trust me completely. Only then would I begin requesting information.

Neither one of us ever ventured to question the nature of our relationship. To me, she was a very valuable asset, an ally who could bring great insight into what lay ahead. When her English began to improve, she indicated that she wished to go to the American Colonies. She had heard great things about the land and people there.

She became a vampire the night we boarded our ship. By the time we landed in Boston, the crew had been reduced by fifteen men. She learned how to take blood from a human quickly and quietly, how to dispose of the body without making a sound, and how to take just a sip or two and compel the human to forget with just a flicker in her coffee-colored eyes.

The first time she experienced a vision after having been changed, she nearly went mad. Everything was enhanced. The things she saw were more clear than ever before. The sounds were deafening. For four days, I implored her to tell me what she'd seen. With a stained linen shift billowing about her like the image of some horrid ghoul, she screamed at me.

She said that she hated me. She hated herself.

To keep the ship's crew quiet about it, I'd had to compel the majority of them. I locked Meekah up for two days in a traveling trunk decorated with real silver emblems of my personal coat of arms. At the end of the second day, I unlocked the trunk.

The shabbily dressed crewman I had brought with me down into the hold was for her. She stared at me silently for several minutes before she bit into him. I had imagined that she would completely drain the man, but she took only a few gulps of his blood.

Then she wiped her mouth, turned to me, and said in a steady tone, "I no trust you. But will tell you what I see. You give what I want."

"Anything you want. Yes." I assured her, relieved that she seemed calm again.

"House in Boston. Big garden."

"Yes. The largest one we can find."

She turned back to the man who had given his blood, grasped his chin gently with her dark calloused fingers and stared into his eyes solemnly, "Forget what has happened here. You go do work again. You forget Meekah drink blood."

111

When he left, she looked at me with a measure of hatred, "You do bad things. I not like that. Meekah good woman."

"I will not force you to do anything."

She sat on a crate full of oranges, "I see new woman. She good to you. Victoria. You change her into blood drinker." Pausing, she held out the remnants of her soiled shift and shook her head, "Big trouble soon. New woman help you."

I leaned forward, "What trouble?"

"I no say. You wait."

Fighting the urge to curse and throw things, I nodded shortly. There was little doubt in my head that what she saw would come to pass. She had been accurate about other things.

So when we got off the ship in Boston, I found her a house with an expansive flowering garden. There were statues and fountains positioned perfectly between the shrubs and carefully tended flowerbeds. I offered the owner three times what the property was worth. His wife cried and pleaded with him to deny me. In the end, Meekah came forward and grasped the woman's hands. She murmured gentle words in her native language while I compelled the husband to sell everything to me for the price I originally offered him.

The very next day, I saw Victoria coming out of a fabric shop. I wasn't positive it was really her in the beginning. She was a slender woman, garbed in threadbare clothing that hung loosely around her petite frame. She had come out of the shop with tears shimmering in her eyes. I remember touching her sleeve and asking if she needed a carriage.

When she turned those eyes on me, I saw that she suffered. It was a raw grating thing that had come up on her over the course of several years; nothing she could correct or control. I discovered later where the pain came from, although it is not a story for me to tell. It is hers alone.

I turned Victoria into a vampire a few days later, after she gave full consent. It was one of the best decisions I ever made. She was unfailingly loyal, grateful for my presence in her life, and incredibly intelligent. Meekah adored her from the first moment they met. I worried occasionally that my seer would try to turn my newest recruit against me. It was unwarranted. Victoria looked upon me as her savior, having rescued her from a life that had ultimately been miserable.

It was a pity that Meekah did not feel the same towards me. But I learned over the decades to placate her, give her what she asked for without too many questions, as long as she told me about her visions. There were times when she refused to reveal what she saw. Back in those days, her gift was so precious to me that I often laughed away her refusals and walked away. Only later did my patience come to its end.

CHAPTER 10 - SARAH

Alex had tried to see me only once, but his respect for Nelly's word was absolute. She had told him that I did not want to see him. He had disappeared into the woods while I watched from my bedroom window. Gone like a dark spirit.

In a few days, I had regained most of my strength. One gray afternoon as I was mucking out the barn stalls, Messenger came walking in through the main barn door. I had not seen much of her at all recently, so I propped the shovel up against the wall and smiled when she stretched her neck forward to sniff at my shirt.

"Have you been staying out of trouble?" I rubbed her forehead in short circling strokes, "Did you finally realize that you missed me? Or did you miss the grain?"

Her ears flicked forward at the word, and I laughed.

"I think I know the answer to that one." I pulled open the half door that led into her stall, "I'll give you a little extra if you get in there without me using a halter on you."

I could have sworn she rolled her eyes. Swinging her head around towards the entrance to the barn, she seemed to consider her options. She gave me another look that conveyed a sense of intense boredom and then stepped lightly into the fresh sawdust of her stall.

Sighing in relief, I pushed the door closed and rested my arms on the top board of the door.

"You're a troublemaker, Sarah."

Messenger suddenly jerked her head up in surprise and let out a snort. When I turned to see what had frightened her, I found the one person I had not ever expected to see on my property again. Trevor Kincaid stood a few feet from me, his face cold with hate and his right arm encased in a thick cast and sling.

"Where is your friend?" He asked.

That was when I saw the Miller brothers loitering outside the barn, looking around anxiously. They did not look particularly threatening. Neither did Trevor, once I got a good look at him. Sure, he was trying to look tough. However, there was clear anxiety exuding from him, and he was being uncharacteristically fidgety.

I sighed and went back to cleaning Lenny's stall. "He's not here, Trevor."

"*What* is he, Sarah?"

Pausing, with my shovel half filled with soiled sawdust, I turned to look at him. There was little doubt in my mind that Trevor wouldn't believe me if I told him the truth. It would also cause a lot of tongues to wag in town, because he would be quick to spread the news that I'd finally gone completely nuts.

"He's a former friend of mine. I don't expect to see him again."

He turned towards his buddies, who seemed to be getting more nervous by the second. I continued scooping manure and hoped he would leave quietly. I should have known better. Strong fingers grabbed my arm and squeezed. Trevor's voice growled against my ear.

"When I find out what I'm up against, I'm going to kill him."

When he did finally walk away, I leaned against the wall and released a long sigh. He was capable of doing some awful things, but Trevor would never survive a real fight against Alex. I decided not to worry about it. There were so many other things going on to drive me crazy. Worrying about Trevor's ridiculous threats was low on my list.

Glancing over at Messenger, I raised my eyebrows, "One more complication."

She snorted, lifted her head and nose up into the air, and curled her lip.

The call from Michael came at 10:30 that evening. I was in my room, getting ready to put on my pajamas when my cell rang. I didn't recognize the number, but it was showing up as a Chicago area code. I didn't know how to feel or what to expect.

"Hello?"

"You were probably thinking you'd never hear from me again."

I sucked in a quick breath of air as I detected the warm tone in his voice.

"Michael? Where are you?"

"Down the road, at the edge of town." He laughed quietly, "I was hoping I'd be able to get in without any help and surprise you in your bed."

My toes curled up in my thick socks.

"I'll be down there in a few minutes. Don't go anywhere." I said. I ended the call and stared at myself in the mirror above my dresser. He was really back. Since I'd released him, I'd had my doubts about whether he would keep his word. My trust in him had just risen by several degrees, and I realized that I couldn't wait to see his face.

With my thoughts focused on the memory of his embrace and the warmth of it, I hopped down the stairs. I almost fell down twice trying to pull on my boots by the back door. By the time I had the truck rattling down the driveway and out onto the road, I was shivering in anticipation.

I was alive. Inside and out. My pulse pounded in my ears, softening the sound of Guns 'N Roses lashing out from the radio. When the headlights illuminated a single dark figure at the side of the road among the bare trees and dead grasses, my heart leapt. I drove up until the truck was twenty feet from him.

He held up one hand to shield the glare of the headlights from his eyes, so I flipped off the lights and shifted the truck into park. I stepped out into the darkness with fierce hope igniting my soul. All I could think was that whatever horrible moments I might live through later, I wanted more than anything to lose myself completely in the magic that was Michael.

I stepped in front of the truck and just watched him for a few moments. I wanted to preserve this moment somehow. I wanted his image etched permanently onto my brain, my flesh, my bones, so that I could look back and see it all again. I didn't want to wait another moment to feel his skin against mine.

He stood there at the edge of the road, the trees immobile and pale behind him. They looked like ghosts waiting expectantly for the next move to be made between the mortals before them. What would they see, those half dead wooden beings waiting patiently for spring to breathe new life into their limbs? Would our little play in this dark landscape be enough to entertain them until the undeniable surge of life sprang forth inside them at the end of March?

Spring seemed very far away. I treasured the cold air around me, the spindly bare trees that reached fruitlessly toward the heavens. At that moment, though, my whole being was focused on the vampire before me; the dark wavy locks of hair that brushed the collar of his long wool coat, the intense hooded eyes that sent shivers through me with every glance. I wanted to hear his voice. I would have begged for a word at that moment.

Instead, I gathered the hollow shell of responsibility around me and asked him, "You pushed the field out this far?"

Silence. Only silence from him, the focus of my every breath, thought, and hope. I ducked my head down and felt a painful slice go through the heart of me. Was he rejecting me? After everything that had happened, after the blood I'd spilled and the tears and the awful battles, was he going to turn his back? That kind of heartlessness would destroy me.

I heard a muttered curse issued from him, and he shifted. Those sky blue eyes closed. His head went back. His fingers curled up into tight, fearless fists. I couldn't drag my gaze away from him. The power behind his every move held me prisoner.

In a few breathless moments, his voice came to me in the numbing breeze.

"If you invite me in right now, it won't just be an invitation into the containment field." It was a simple statement of fact. He wasn't asking me a question. He was declaring what he knew to be the startling truth.

My breath rose in a cloud before me over and over again, as I contemplated this undeniable path we had both stepped onto and rushed along without much planning, without enough caution or judgment. And there it was. Such things happened.

"You won't deny me?" I whispered.

He didn't laugh. He moved towards me with guileless determination, his expression unreadable. A few feet away, he halted and regarded me with a serious expression. It was impossible to see either hesitation or anticipation in the smooth angles of his face.

"Deny you? You honestly think I can do that?" He swore again, the words floating away in the wind before I could discern their meaning.

I turned inward, examining what had come before. I thought about Alex and what he'd done to me, how he'd made me feel so weak. Would it be the same with Michael? Would he infuse me with some of his own power? Would he be able to deny himself the taste of my blood once we had crossed every other boundary? How much control did he have over his desires?

Always doubting. I was tired of the questions blazing through me, sick of being so cautious around him. I wanted to throw myself into the fate that had been assigned to me and let everything fall where it may. I couldn't control anyone but myself. If something terrible happened, would it be my fault? I didn't deserve to put my entire life on hold, dreading what might come.

I dropped my mantle of doubt on the cold road, and I pushed my shoulders back.

"Come in, Michael. Please." Strong words, coming from me.

With his jaw clenched tightly, he stared at me. Then one of his hands came forward tentatively, as if testing some unseen boundary. There was no barrier, so he stepped towards me. The breeze picked up, tousling his ebony hair.

There was a significant change in the air around us. It felt colder. Before his arms came around me, before his mouth descended down onto mine for the first time, I saw the first snowflakes begin to drift down towards us like little angels bestowing a blessing. And that's the moment when I knew where my heart belonged.

It was a chaste little token, that light kiss. His lips were smooth, full, and gentle. The heat of his mouth against mine was heart wrenching, and I felt the muscles in my legs go weak. He had me fully supported in the way he held me; I could have gone totally limp and he would still have me.

His mouth moved down over one side of my jaw, nibbling at my flesh and stroking it. I opened my eyes, my head tilting back. His arms were firm around my waist, his mouth fused to my neck. And the snow was falling on both of us. They were tender, delicate little sculptures of ivory perfection, perching on the fibers of his coat and the long ebony waves of his hair. I wanted to remember this moment forever.

There was increasing strength coming from his arms around me and the pressure of his mouth on my skin. An image flashed across my consciousness that made my blood run cold. Again, I saw Alex kneeling on my bed, his mouth working to pull my blood from me. I saw the way his mouth looked as he pulled away, dripping with crimson. There was no stopping the shudder that ran through my entire body. Michael felt it immediately, and to his credit, he did not mistake it for lust. Somehow, he could sense my fear.

He withdrew his mouth, loosened his grip around me. I heard a deep forlorn sigh issue from the depths of his chest, and his head sagged in defeat.

"You are one hell of temptation, Sarah." His lips tasted mine once more, very gently, before he began to steer me towards the truck. "Come on. You'll freeze out here."

I rubbed my hands together and shot him a grateful look, "Thank you."

"For what? Accosting you in the middle of the road during the season's first snow?" There was a terribly charming gleam in his light blue eyes.

"No. For stopping before you got carried away." He had opened the driver's door and was watching me carefully.

Suddenly nervous, I stammered, "Not that you were the only one who was feeling aroused."

One corner of his incredible mouth quirked up in amusement. He seemed to be genuinely pleased to have turned me into a bumbling idiot. Jerk. I huffed and threw myself into the driver's seat. Without another word, he went to the other side and got in. As I was trying to make a U-turn on the road, I felt his gaze going over me.

Having anyone look at me in that way made me crazy. With him, the feeling was multiplied a thousand times. Having turned the truck around successfully, I decided to take a different approach. I could be direct when the situation called for it. Whenever I was feeling embarrassed, that was how I could keep things under control.

"Tell me something." I snapped. "Exactly how old are you?" I kept my eyes on the road. The snow was coming down steadily. Big, fluffy frozen sparks of light where the headlights shone on them in the darkness.

"As a human, I was born in a small Greek village in 1659. So, technically, I'm over three hundred and fifty years old." He said it in a light tone, and I dared to look over at him.

126

"How old were you when you were turned into a vampire?"

"Twenty-seven years old."

I waited for more information, but he said nothing else about being turned. Frustrated with the lack of pertinent facts about him, I gritted my teeth. Being mysterious might have taken him a long way with many women, but not with me. I still wanted answers.

"Can all vampires be out in the daylight? I thought it burned them or something." I couldn't seem to keep the sarcastic, bitchy edge toned down. It didn't matter. Michael wasn't offended in the least.

"Some of us are capable of doing so, but it is a very uncomfortable situation to be in. Some vampires are able to use crystals to ward off the pain." He reached into one of the pockets of his coat and drew out a small red stone, "Victoria gave me this before she left. It came in quite handy the day you were attacked."

Attacked. Right. I sighed and made the turn into the driveway. The tires crunched over the gravel, like bones being crushed beneath us. I didn't want to think about Alex, but his face kept flashing back to me. His shining golden hair, his charming smile, the way he

127

made me completely helpless after we'd made love. I hated remembering it all, because at the end, he was looking at me with my blood smeared across his face, and I was lying prone on the stained sheets with my life draining away.

Fighting the urge to shiver, I parked the truck back by the garage and looked over at Michael. His dark eyebrows were creased in an expression that conveyed intense concentration. I placed a hand on his arm.

"Sorry for snapping at you."

He waved a hand at me in dismissal, "Your temper is good to see. I'd rather have you screaming at me than pale and motionless on a bed." His eyes skipped away in a guilty gesture.

"Wait a minute..." I stared at him, my mind spinning with the sudden realization that Michael could actually discern exactly what I was thinking.

"You're a mind reader?"

He pulled that old arrogant mask down over himself with practiced ease, "I'm a powerful vampire. I have many gifts."

I snorted, "Okay..." As I reached over to open my door, he suddenly grasped my arm.

When I turned to look at him, he was shaking his head. His eyes were closed, but his grip on me got a little tighter. Again, I felt a strange pulling sensation that had nothing to do with where he had his strong fingers wrapped around my forearm.

"Michael, what are you doing?"

His eyes opened, and his hand dropped away from me. He turned from me to look out into the flying snow for a moment before he said anything.

When his voice sounded beside me, I felt chilled to the bone.

"If I can find a way, I will see him dead. He will suffer for bringing you so close to death." Then he opened the door, and a thousand icy flakes of snow swirled in towards me. I felt lost among them, as powerless against the currents as they were. I watched one tiny snowflake descend slowly, without a clear direction, onto the surface of my denim-clad thigh.

It disappeared so swiftly, leaving nothing behind. I began to worry that my fate might be the same.

S.J. Wright

CHAPTER 11 - SARAH

Nelly was waiting at the front door in her old flannel housecoat when we got up onto the porch.

"Oh, thank goodness." She held the door open for both of us, "I wasn't sure what was going on. I heard your truck start and was worried you might have headed over to Bill's."

"Who's Bill?" Michael inquired, his eyes moving from Nelly back to me.

I rolled my eyes at him, "Bill's is a bar I go to every now and then."

"The tavern?"

"Yeah, I guess." I forgot sometimes that he'd been buried in the middle of nowhere since 1945.

"Michael, some packages showed up for you yesterday. They're out on the back porch." Nelly said, pushing the front door closed behind her and locking it.

He nodded, "Victoria said she was sending some things to me."

"Blood?" The hopeful expression on Nelly's face was almost comical. I turned my face away and covered my smile with one hand.

Michael caught up one of Nelly's hands and put it on his bent arm, "Lead the way, dear lady. We shall see." He left me with a wink, sweeping out of the room with my elderly housekeeper on his arm.

I shook my head, smiling again. Then the cell phone rang that I had stashed in my coat pocket. Pulling it out, I pressed the receive button before checking the Caller ID.

"This is Sarah."

"There is a very important individual who wants to meet you, Miss Wood." An unfamiliar male voice. That probably wasn't a good thing.

"Okay. Who is this?" I demanded.

"Who I am is of no consequence." He replied calmly, "The person who wants to meet you would like to make sure that you will be available two days from now."

"What is this about?"

There was a moment's pause, "It is regarding the vampire in your custody. Michael Graviano."

I grew very still. I'd never heard Michael's last name before. It sounded Greek, I supposed. I peeked around the corner and saw that Michael was on the back porch with Nelly, opening the packages he'd received from Victoria. Could this caller be someone from the council? Had they discovered I'd released Michael?

"What about him?" I asked.

"There are some who say he was incarcerated without good reason. My employer would like to meet with you, two nights from now in Indianapolis. I will be calling you again with the place and time. It would not be wise of you to share this with anyone." There was a barely audible click over the line and then silence.

I stared at the phone, thinking furiously. Who could want to meet me? If it were someone trying to free Michael based on real evidence, I knew I had to hear them out. Of course, he would never approve of me going alone. Deciding to keep the information to myself, I slipped the phone back into my pocket.

"Who was that?" Michael had crept up behind me without me realizing it.

"Just Katie." I lied.

I felt his breath in my ear. It created a riot of hot sparks across my cheeks and neck.

"You're not a skilled liar, my love." He grasped my arms gently and turned me to face him. I nearly melted into the floor at the admonishment written across his face and the way his clear blue eyes studied me.

"I'm sorry." I sighed, "But it's not going to be easy to just put all my trust in you right away." Reaching up, I tucked back a lock of hair that had fallen down over his ear, "You are a blood-sucking beast of the night, right?"

"Hmm." He wasn't satisfied with my teasing, but he dropped the subject.

"Hey, what happened with Luanna? Is she still in the caves?"

"She is still there. I need to get some answers out of her about Gunter." He said.

I didn't want him to leave, but he was moving toward the front door. Craving an embrace, a quick kiss, a whispered word, I grabbed his arm, "You're going?"

He nodded shortly, glancing down at my hand, "I have things I need to take care of." Brightening suddenly, he flashed a grin, "Don't worry, angel. I'll be back."

Arrogant, as always. I took my hand off his arm and shrugged. "Oh, that's fine. Don't hurry back."

"Oh, no. Don't play the tough girl with me." He whispered the words in my ear, his lips grazing my earlobe, "We both know that the other cares. No more pretending."

Did he have any idea how hard that was for me? To just let go and not worry about protecting myself? Perhaps he knew. Maybe he thought he could change me, make me trust him. He brushed my cheek with his lips and slipped out the door before I could say anything more.

I wandered into the kitchen. It was lit only by the light over the sink. Nelly sat at the kitchen table, sipping at a cup of tea.

"He said he'd be back for the packages later." She said.

I nodded absently, "Sure."

My emotions were at war inside me. Everything that had happened with Alex had left me totally off balance. I wasn't sure how to handle Michael, now that I knew he wanted me. He had earned my trust by returning to the inn, but what if he had some other agenda? I was terrified he would end up turning away from me.

"Penny for your thoughts." Nelly said.

I nibbled on my thumbnail, looking out the window into the fathomless woods beyond the backyard. After a moment, I turned to her. "Would it be a really bad thing if I fell for Michael?"

She pursed her lips and raised her gray eyebrows, "It could be." She didn't seem very surprised by my question, I'd noticed. She patted the chair next to her, so I sat down and crossed my arms on the tabletop.

"He's difficult." I said.

"Yes, he is that." She replied calmly, taking another sip from her steaming cup of Earl Grey.

"And he's egotistical."

"I believe he can be that way sometimes."

A heavy sigh escaped me, and I lowered my head into my arms. "This is so messed up."

"I'm going to tell you what my Aunt Lucille told me when I first asked her about love."

I turned to look at her without much enthusiasm, "What's that?"

"Keep your head above your heart. God put it there for a reason. And don't be a whiney little asshole." She grinned over at me.

Laughter exploded out of me, "She actually said that?"

Nelly nodded wisely and drank the last of her tea. "Yes, indeed. Lucille gave some good advice sometimes, but she could be a cold-hearted bitch."

S.J. Wright

CHAPTER 12 - MICHAEL

None of it had gone as planned. I was to have made the call and then lured her outside of the boundary. I had been caught up in the hope that lit her entire face. None of the speech I had prepared made it past my lips. All I could do was question my own purposes as I watched her. Her hair fell around her face like a shimmering amber veil, lifting and undulating with the wind. Her eyes were wide with anticipation, glittering in the meager light of the evening.

In the centuries since I had become one of the undead, I had never wanted a mortal woman as intensely as I craved Sarah. She was the ultimate temptation. Not just the breathtakingly delicious blood that flowed through her veins. I had the pleasure of tasting a little of it when I healed the wounds that Alex had inflicted on her. What had me entranced was the strength of her convictions, the saucy way she tossed harsh words at those she feared the most. Her courage, her voice, her hidden insecurities.

Every little fanciful thought that had ever passed through my mind about the girl suddenly rushed over me as I stood there in the darkness on that road. She stood there, hiding nothing. The expression she wore tore holes through me with its honesty. I might have drawn her away at that moment. It would have only taken a gentle word or two, but I felt powerless.

I have had many women. In the beginning, it was always about the blood and satisfying that thirst that drives all vampires. But we are capable of much more. I learned how to use my words, my eyes, my hands and my mouth to bring the kind of pleasure to a woman that she had never before experienced. There were times when all I really wanted was the coppery warmth of blood in my mouth, flowing down my throat. However, I preferred to be discrete with my feeding. If a woman was rendered nearly unconscious due to the effects of an incredible orgasm, she was less likely to feel alarmed when my teeth sank into her flesh. Compulsion is one of my abilities, but I use it sparingly. Perhaps it is one of my few moral qualms.

Sarah's sudden vulnerability left me stunned. When I crossed over the boundary and took her into my arms, it was the strangest sensation. No one who knew me would have believed how easily I tossed away my chance at freedom. The deadly vampire, Michael Graviano, drawn back into imprisonment due to the heartrending expression on the face of a human. Impossible.

When I left the house, the snow had begun to taper off. As I walked slowly down the lane towards the meadow, I drew from my coat pocket the cell phone that Victoria had insisted I purchase. It had taken only a few moments for me to flip through the little operating manual, memorizing the button functions, how to set up the address book, how to set up my voicemail box and how to delete call information. That last one might prove to be very important.

The technological advances of this new century were alarming. I wasn't opposed to learning as much as I could, but learning to drive a vehicle was something different. Trusting a machine to move safely at seventy miles per hour was beyond me. Vampires are not technically immortal. There are ways to destroy us. Decapitation due to a high-speed collision would definitely put an end to my endless desires and numerous sins.

I tapped the necessary keys to bring up Victoria's cell phone number and hit the send button.

"Michael."

"I'm back inside the containment field."

She didn't seem at all surprised, "I know. Meekah told me it would happen that way. What's going on there?"

Victoria and I had not discussed the unusual relationship I had with Sarah. We discussed strategy in regards to the council, in particular, Isaiah. We had talked about Alex and how his powers had developed. She had said quite simply that she liked Sarah, admired her spirit, and felt that she would turn out to be a valuable ally.

I didn't share with Victoria the dreams I'd had about the girl. I'd neglected to mention the heat that infused me whenever she was close. I said nothing about the way she aroused every carnal instinct within me to rise up and roar with fruitless anger at the hopeless situation in which we were mired.

But Victoria was no fool. Meekah could have told her anything. My faith in Victoria was well placed. She would never betray me, never rise against me in any fashion. Meekah was questionable, but not Victoria.

"Sarah is safe. I did see Alex once outside of town, but he got away."

She sighed, "He's going to be a problem, Michael."

"I know. Has Meekah said anything more?"

"Nothing useful. She wants to leave."

Pausing at the entrance to the meadow, I cursed. I needed to know that Meekah was on my side and wouldn't hesitate to provide information if I needed it. She was incredibly hard to please, and I didn't trust her. She might already be working against me.

"Let her go. But keep an eye on her for a day or two."

"You think Isaiah may have recruited her?"

"It has crossed my mind. I wish I had some kind of leverage with her." I said.

Victoria chuckled, "Reminds me of old times."

With a low grunt, I acknowledged her sharp memory. "She's a thorn in my side, Vic. There's no controlling her, and there's not a damn thing I can do about it."

"You know how I admire her spirit, Michael. But you're right. Maybe it's time you washed your hands of her." She paused a moment, and her next words were said with genuine alarm. "If she ever truly wanted revenge, she would have all the ammunition available to destroy you."

I approached the huge boulders leisurely, "I know. That's part of the reason why I haven't completely let her go. Between the threat that she represents and the power she holds with those visions, it would be in our best interest to keep her as happy as possible."

That's when I realized I was no longer alone in the clearing. A familiar old scent was wafting through the chilling winds, "I've got company, Vic. I'll phone you tomorrow." I pressed the end button and walked around the largest of the three huge rocks.

A decrepit, gray figure of a creature was leaning weakly against the rocky surface. It lifted its head with a groan and eyed me with familiar black eyes. The thing coughed and wretched, producing nothing from inside but a cloud of gray dust that was taken up on the winds without touching the ground.

"Convenient timing, Jones." I said with a grin.

The reply was a grinding mumble that would have frightened the hardiest of old souls, "Either go to hell or give me blood, you worthless old Yank." There was the tiniest hint of a British accent somewhere in there.

"We're already in hell, my friend." I replied brightly. "Welcome to Indiana."

Then I plunged my sharp canines into my wrist and held out my arm to him.

S.J. Wright

CHAPTER 13 - SARAH

The lights of the city beckoned me forward. They illuminated the busy streets and sidewalks in downtown Indianapolis just as they had the first time I'd come into the city with my father when I was just ten years old.

We had come there for the Circle of Lights festival. I remembered that Katie had been sick with the flu the day after Thanksgiving, and Nelly knew I had been pleading with my father to take me downtown. Some of my friends at school had been bragging that they went to the festival downtown every year. Nelly urged my dad to take me while she looked after Katie. It was one of the few times that he had taken time away from the inn just for me.

We had to park far away from the monument. I remember how he carried me on his shoulders for part of the way and how I tickled his ears when I was up there, looking out at all of the people and lights. It was like a whole new world, this busy place so far away from the peaceful fields and forests of home.

This time, it was no festival I was attending, but an important meeting. It was a meeting with someone powerful. Katie had returned the journal to me one day when we had lunch on the west side of Indy. She didn't ask many questions that day, but she was in a hurry to get back to school for a class. I was planning to add an entry to the journal after the meeting. I wanted to record as much as I could remember, just as my grandfather had done after he had attended these kinds of functions.

Michael didn't know about my plans that evening. I hadn't even told Nelly what I was really doing. She had gone to Greenwood again, this time to visit her brother who was recovering from pneumonia and was still in the hospital.

So it had been a good time for mulling over the events that had occurred over the past few weeks, as I drove north towards the city. The traffic wasn't too heavy that evening. The snow that had fallen several days ago had quickly melted, and we had experienced a short warming trend.

The voicemail message that I'd received on my cell phone stated that I was expected to attend a meeting at

The St. Elizabeth Hotel in downtown Indianapolis. I glanced at the clock on the dashboard of the truck. If I could find a decent spot in the parking garage, I would still be a few minutes early.

I walked into the marble-floored lobby not knowing what to expect. I hadn't been downtown in a very long time, and never had I been into that particular hotel. It was classically elegant, decorated in muted earth tones with overstuffed leather sofas and glass-topped tables. There were large potted plants in every corner that looked well tended and gave a natural air to the lobby.

Approaching the front desk, I smiled at the clerk. He was a young black man with an impeccable smile and welcoming expression.

"How may I help you?"

"My name is Sarah Wood. I was supposed to meet someone here." I tugged nervously at one of the sleeves of the new black blazer I wore. I hated wearing the things, but my father had told me years ago that a black blazer and slacks were classic business wear. That had been before I'd dropped out of business school, and he was attempting to give me some advice about proper interview attire.

"Yes, Miss Wood. Mrs. Latimer is expecting you. She is down the hall, in the Venetian Business Suite. Would you like me to show you?"

"No, thank you. Just point me in the right direction."

Mrs. Latimer was expecting me. The person who'd called my cell phone had been a man. I was sure of that much. But he hadn't left his name or the names of who I was supposed to meet.

I headed in the direction in which the clerk had pointed and began looking at the names on the brass plates next to each intricately carved door. An elegantly dressed elderly couple passed me, and I smiled politely at them.

Out of my element and hating what I was wearing, my frazzled state of mind caused me to miss the suite, and I had to turn back when I reached the end of the hall and an exit that led to a side alley. Finally, I saw the nameplate I'd been looking for and reached for the doorknob.

Whoever waited at the other side of that door knew about Michael. They knew about the role I'd inherited. How much information should I withhold if the questions became too pointed? I took a deep breath to calm myself, turned the knob, and pushed the door open.

The suite was occupied by only one person. It was an elderly lady with stylishly cut silver hair, and she was smiling at me as I entered. She sat at a small round table that was covered with a pristine white tablecloth, a pitcher of water and one glass.

"I'm sorry," I started badly, glancing behind me towards the door. "I believe I'm in the wrong room."

"You're in the right place, my dear." Her voice was gentle and soothing, carrying with it a hint of an Italian accent. I noticed then that her eyes were black as ink, gleaming at me in a certain amount of personal amusement.

She wore a platinum ring on one hand with a huge ruby in the center. It flashed at me menacingly as she waved me towards the empty chair across from her, "Please have a seat, Sarah. I'm very eager to talk with you."

Uneasily, I lowered myself into the richly upholstered chair across from her. Her eyes made me shiver. She settled back into her chair and tilted her head as she looked at me. My heart was fluttering madly in my chest. Suddenly, I felt the need to run away.

"Let me introduce myself. I am Theodora." There was regality in that voice. It was impossible to deny that this woman was quite powerful. Just the quiet dignity of the way she sat was enough to prove that point. She held herself as a queen might.

"It's nice to meet you." I replied, still not able to look her in the face. Fear was still rising inside me.

"You are afraid." She said lightly. "There's no reason for that, my dear. I have no intention of doing you any harm."

"Are you a vampire?"

She nodded and smiled a little sadly, "Yes, I am. But probably not the kind you might expect."

"There are different kinds of vampires?" This was news to me.

Waving a pale hand, she shook her head, "We'll not delve into those matters at this point. Let us discuss your current role."

I considered her statement and the situation as a whole. I was in an unfamiliar place with a very dangerous stranger who had just admitted to being a vampire. Anger ignited inside me like a bright fire.

"Let's just cut through the bullshit, okay?" I demanded.

Her expression went from benevolence to pure shock in an instant. Her ebony eyes widened, and her lips opened.

I leaned towards her, "I don't know what you want from me. But you haven't given me any indication of who you really are, and I'm getting tired of being the last one to know what the hell is going on with all this vampire crap."

After a brief silence, I heard her chuckle in delight. She tipped her head back and rolled her eyes towards the ceiling, "My heavens! You certainly have some spirit, don't you?"

Mollified a little, I turned away and crossed my arms. At least she hadn't attacked me.

"Oh, Sarah. You are a balm to my bitter old soul." She rested her arms on the table and regarded me with a friendly grin. "We are going to get along perfectly well. Let me begin by telling you exactly who I am and why I've requested to see you."

I watched her with suspicion as she began, but as she began to tell me her real story I found myself leaning forward, eager to hear more and feeling a fragile connection beginning to form between us. She told me of her childhood, growing up as the daughter of an actress. When I began to ask a question, she would shake her head. I wanted to know where and when. How old was she? When had she been turned?

She explained that she'd turned to prostitution when she was very young and then had become a performer. Men were easy to manipulate, in her opinion. A woman only had to appeal to their most basic physical demands to be granted access to immense power. With a faint sigh, she recalled how she met the man who would eventually become her husband.

"He was too handsome for his own good. Justin was from a very powerful family and used to having

154

his own way. He was given exactly what he wanted. Until he met me."

She smiled brilliantly, thinking back to those golden days of courtship. I could detect the love she had for him, the dedication that grew as the years went by. It was written on her face like ink on a page, bold and unashamed.

"Now, let us discuss Michael."

Inwardly, I hesitated. I needed to know more before I divulged anything about the vampire in my custody.

"Theodora…" I began slowly.

"No! My goodness, child. Don't call me that. We are going to be friends, so you may call me Teddy."

I smiled back at her, "Teddy."

Suddenly, it was as if a shadow had fallen over her. Her perfectly arched eyebrows drew together over her black eyes, and she became very still. Her gaze was not focused on me, but something far away and beyond my understanding. Whatever it was, it held her immobile for a few moments. Then she looked directly at me.

"You must go." She said quickly.

I stood, feeling frustrated and alarmed, "Why?"

"You were followed." She rose quickly from her seat and approached me with worry firmly fixed on her pale face, "We cannot be found here together. The Council was not to know that I was meeting you tonight."

"I thought you were with the Council!"

"I am a part of it. But there are those who would destroy me for interfering." She grasped my arm gently and moved me towards the door. "Do not go home right away. They will be expecting that."

"Who? Other members of the Council?"

She shook her head firmly, "There's no time to explain it to you now. Now listen to me. There is a pub one block east of here called Fanny's. Go in there and wait for twenty minutes or so. That should be enough time for me to lead them away from here."

"Teddy, why am I in danger? What have I done?" I asked, desperation rising hot and fast inside my chest.

"It's not what you've done." She opened the door and looked both ways down the hall before turning back to me. Her face was hard and her black eyes glittered with fear.

"They want to punish you for what you are *going* to do."

S.J. Wright

CHAPTER 14 - MICHAEL

Images began playing in my mind. At first, they were hazy and confusing. Sarah entering a room by herself, sitting down at a table. I had been reading one of the computer manuals that Victoria had sent me, trying to get through the last few chapters of instruction on how to set up a private discussion forum. It would prove to be both a curse and a blessing in the months that followed.

The wind was not as cold as it had been. On top of the largest gatestone, I tested the air with my enhanced sense of smell. Sadie was nearby, moving through the trees to the north of the meadow following the scent of a rabbit. I turned my gaze from the words on the page to the trees where her scent was wafting from. Concentrating, I narrowed my focus and searched for her golden fur. There she was, sniffing at the ground and moving along at an excited pace.

"You'll never catch that rabbit." I said loudly, grinning at her.

Her head shot up, and she stared at me curiously with her warm brown eyes. There was a fragile truce between the two of us since I'd revealed myself to Sarah. There was much more to Sadie than just the friendly, goofy Golden Retriever exterior that humans might see. It hadn't been pure coincidence that the young dog had wandered onto the property four years earlier.

"Jones."

"What?"

I gestured towards Sadie, who had begun to stare pointedly in our direction. My recently arisen, redheaded companion looked at the dog briefly from his lounging position on the second Gatestone then went back to reading a copy of Twilight that Victoria had included with the computer books as a jest.

Aiden Jones had been a captain in the English Navy back in the middle of the 18th century. He had been turned by a particularly malevolent female vampire while crossing the English Channel to France in 1783. Her name was Amanda Winston, and she was one of the most vicious vampires I'd ever encountered.

I'd found Jones washed up on the rocky shore north of Calais, almost completely drained of blood and half dead from lying out in the sun for three days. Curious about him and his circumstances, I gave him some of my blood and moved him in to a guest bedroom at my country home on the outskirts of the city of Calais.

As it turned out, he was an interesting fellow. For an Englishman, he was a rather large specimen. He stood nearly seven feet tall, had the muscles of a gladiator and the demeanor of a demon when provoked. He had the red hair and drinking capacity of an Irishman, though he adamantly claimed to be English born.

Our friendship was based on common interests. He was enamored with French impressionist art and loose women. We'd spent three years as captain and first mate aboard a pirate ship in the Caribbean, during which we became exceedingly wealthy. When I grew bored with the sailing, I went back to Paris. We met up again in New York in 1908. He stuck with Victoria and me through many tremulous years, and due to the fact that he'd witnessed me turning Alex, he was deemed a coconspirator in my crime. Therefore, we both ended up trapped within the containment field.

I heard Jones groan and slap his hand against the surface of the stone.

"What a bloody fabrication!" He exclaimed.

I chuckled, "Which chapter are you reading?"

"Edward just showed that dim-witted wench how he looks in the sunlight."

"Ah, yes. He doesn't project a very masculine image, does he?"

"Masculine, my arse! He's bent as a nine-pound note!" Jones tossed the book to the ground below the Gatestone, leaped down upon it with a sneer, and proceeded to piss upon it.

I shook my head. It wouldn't do any good to try to placate the man. He had his Irish up.

A darkness began to settle over my mood rather suddenly. Incoming images flashed across my consciousness like a swarm of bees towards a hive. Flashes of Sarah's sweet face, an unfamiliar building in a city, and a very familiar female vampire.

Theodora. I rose from my position on the rock and tried to concentrate. I sensed danger. Surprise. Then

162

an image of Katie emerged from somewhere. She was wearing a provocative red dress and stumbling into a low-lit tavern, a cell phone grasped in one hand. She moved across the room towards two people who were arguing near the restrooms. She slid a hand up the arm of the man, her red fingernails entwined in his blond hair like snakes as she looked at the other woman.

Sarah. Rage launched me upward into the sky. When I hit the ceiling, a snarl ripped from my throat. I couldn't go to her. It escalated the anger churning inside me, the realization that I was powerless to help. Alex could kill both of them with a flick of his fingers. I'd felt the power he was capable of. There had to be a way to get some kind of help to Sarah.

Drifting back to the ground, I saw Jones had gone completely still. The copy of Twilight lay forgotten in the dirt. Wrenching the cell phone from my pocket with a curse, I wondered yet again how far I could stretch the containment field wall.

Victoria picked up on the first ring.

"Michael."

"Where are you?"

163

"Carmel. I'm driving back from Chicago." She'd heard the tremor in my tone, "What's happened?"

"Did Meekah say anything at all about Sarah being downtown?" I asked, already on the road that led to town, followed closely by Jones.

"No, she said nothing like that. Are you sure she's there? Do you know why?" I heard the engine rev in the background and the squealing of tires.

"She didn't say anything about it at all. But I've seen something. I'm fairly certain she's run into Alex."

"Shit."

"Exactly."

I watched Jones try to punch through the invisible bubble that was keeping us from moving further down the road. There was an iridescent spark of power where his fist connected, but he wasn't able to stretch it. He threw a string of curses into the still night air and rubbed his hand as if in pain. Looking around, I realized we were in the exact spot that Sarah had stood several nights ago when I kissed her for the first time.

Imagining Alex with his hands on her was tortuous in the extreme. If I didn't get some kind of help, there was a good possibility that he would not only get his hands on her again, but also possibly turn her into one of us. Sarah, a vampire. There was no way I could allow him to go that far. I was willing to do anything to stop it from happening.

"Vic, I want you to call Isaiah's people and set up a meeting. Tell them I'm ready to deal."

She went quiet for so long, I thought we'd lost the connection. Finally, she sighed.

"Oh, Michael. I don't think this is a good idea."

It was a rare thing for Vic to try to dissuade me from a decision. Her trust in my judgment had always seemed infinite, giving me the kind of courage I needed in times of trouble. When things were uncertain, when our lives were at stake, I knew I could count on her to back me up. No matter what.

"Listen to me, Victoria. I have to find a way to stop Alex. Isaiah has the power to do that."

"What are you going to offer them?"

Hesitation gripped me. What Isaiah really wanted was my ultimate surrender and bloody demise. Could I give myself up in exchange for securing the safety of Sarah and her sister? It was a frightening path, and there was no guarantee that Isaiah would keep his word. There was even a possibility that he didn't have the power to take on Alex.

"I've got to try, Vic."

"You want them to come to the farm?"

"Yes. Jones is finally awake. He can help if we need it."

She took a shallow breath, and I knew I'd hit a nerve. Victoria and I had never been lovers. But she had fallen very much in love with the Captain. Jones had always been a little resistant towards her emotional attachment. I'd suspected that he probably felt the same way towards her, but he was far too appreciative of her friendship to upset the balance of things.

"Any idea exactly where Sarah is right now?" She was trying to get back to business, and I was relieved.

"I'm not sure. Maybe she'll answer her cell phone if she sees your number come up."

"Will you try to call her as well?"

"Yes. Let me know." I hit the end button and turned to Jones. "We need a plan, my friend."

His wide shoulders rose in an exasperated shrug, "Do I have a choice?"

S.J. Wright

CHAPTER 15 - SARAH

I was a basket case. I kept seeing Katie's face and how dead her eyes looked as Alex lowered his head and pressed his lips against hers. Any evidence that my sister still existed had been wiped away by Alex's compulsion. At least, I assumed that's what it was. I'd been reading up on various vampire myths and stories over the previous few weeks. What I'd discovered had been confusing, interesting and probably fabrications. I knew that some of the myths weren't true, but I hadn't really had much of a chance to discuss my findings with Michael.

Sitting in the passenger seat of Victoria's sleek black Mercedes, I dashed away the lingering tears and tried not to think about Katie. Or Alex. But it was overwhelming, what I'd just been through. What I'd seen.

"You want to talk about it?" Victoria asked.

I shook my head, "No."

"I think you should."

Turning my head, I gazed at her. How could she always be so composed? Was it a vampire thing? I guess I should have felt grateful for her help, given the fact that I was in no condition to drive after seeing Alex and Katie together at the bar.

"Michael cares for you very much, you know." Her words were spoken carefully, with eloquent precision. "He has never been willing to sacrifice so much for a human."

"What do you mean?"

She pressed her lips together for a moment, as if to stifle the answer. When she did speak again, it was in a cold tone.

"He saved me. When my human life had become unbearable, there he was. He offered me a way out of the misery." She kept her cool hazel eyes fixed on the road before us. "Everything I now have, I owe to Michael."

That was loyalty. I recognized it.

"He is lucky to count you as a friend." I said softly.

She glanced over at me with a hint of caution in her expression, "He's not perfect. You know he's not.

But he's capable of great things. I once saw him rescue an entire family from a rogue vampire. There is a great deal of good left in him."

"I certainly hope that's true."

"You doubt it."

"Sometimes I don't know what to think of him." I pressed two fingers against the glass of my window, feeling the cold smooth surface but seeing nothing. My mind was somewhere else. With Alex and Katie. With Michael.

She merged onto the interstate that led south.

He was waiting on the road with a man I'd never seen before. As we drew closer to the two of them, I realized that the other one probably wasn't human. I heard Victoria's quick intake of breath and saw her eyes come alive when she saw the two of them. I realized a few minutes later that it was the redhead who had caused this transformation in her.

When I got out of the car, all I wanted was Michael's embrace. The smooth tips of his fingers against my face, drawing away the pain. I didn't care about the tension that was riding the air between Victoria and the stranger. I didn't care about the mascara running down my cheeks.

For just a miniscule moment in time, I saw relief wash over him completely when he saw me. The tightness around his amazing eyes relaxed, smoothing out that little line between his eyebrows. His generous mouth softened, his lips parted slightly. Those broad shoulders fell. It was a slice of naked vulnerability as he watched me come towards him.

He had probably been hoping I might have missed it. But in my head, I mapped it all out like a picture that I could hold and look back on when the need might arise. I suddenly realized that no matter what games he thought he might be playing, he really loved me. In spite of his vampire's nature.

Michael *loved* me.

"Are you alright?" He had quickly morphed into the guise of a concerned acquaintance.

Stopping a few feet from him, I nodded. He glanced from Victoria to the redhead.

"Sarah, this is Captain Aiden Jones. He's just risen from the caves."

I nodded at the captain awkwardly. There would time later for pleasantries, I told myself. The captain gave me a firm nod in acknowledgement. His attention was fixed on something else as well. Victoria had stepped out of the car.

Her eyes didn't move from the captain's face when she spoke to me, "You'll need to invite me back in, Sarah."

"Actually, I think Jones might enjoy a little freedom." Michael said, casting a penetrating glance towards the two of them.

"Oh." I nodded, understanding him and beginning to feel my blood heat up. "Victoria, why don't you take him down to Bloomington?"

"Are you sure, Michael? What about Alex?" She asked.

My blood went cold just hearing her say his name. My head fell as I recalled the events of the evening. My fear for Katie, the loss of her, weighed me down. Would I ever get my sister back after tonight? It was clear that Alex was just using her to get to me. Some kind of payback for turning him away or something like that. Then a single thought broke through everything, releasing a storm of guilt that hovered over me like a horrible dark faceless monster.

Was he getting his revenge for what I'd done? Allowing them to turn him into a vampire?

Michael knew immediately that something had changed. He reached my side with unbelievable speed and pulled me against him, "Sarah, give permission to the captain to go."

"You may go, Captain Jones." I said haltingly, the rising tide of guilt drew a little sob from me at the end of the required statement.

They left in Victoria's car. Michael watched them drive away.

His eyes, when they came to rest on me, were swimming with serious contemplation that I found comforting. I didn't want his sarcasm or his entrapping innuendos at that point. I didn't want pity either. I just wanted him near me.

Calmly, he took my hand and began leading me up the road towards the driveway. His fingers were warm. When I glanced over at him, he kept his eyes on the road. We walked together down that dark road with the future looming gray and unknown ahead of us.

Inside my head, despite the comforting touch of Michael's skin against mine, I began to feel oddly detached. There was a darkness blooming all around me that held no light, no love, and hope at all. My feet moved, and I kept drawing in breaths of air, but my brain was being consumed by something I couldn't fight against.

S.J. Wright

CHAPTER 16 - MICHAEL

She sat silently in the window seat of the study for hours. I waited for her to cry, to rail against Alex and his changeable appetites, even to curse me for my inability to stop what was happening to her sister. Her face was without definable expression. Her beautiful eyes were lifeless, like a doll.

Nelly called twice while I was there and left two messages. Sarah didn't respond to the ringing of the phone. In fact, she responded to nothing. Sadie crept past me at one point and pushed her wet nose against Sarah's hand. Even the dog received no response from her.

Desperate and angry, I fled from the room and called Victoria.

"She won't speak." I growled as soon as she answered.

Victoria was hesitant, and I wondered if I might have interrupted something between her and Jones.

"I'm sorry. Is this a *bad time*?" The words were a hiss through my teeth.

"No, it's fine. She hasn't said anything about what happened?"

"Not a damn word. Were you able to get anything out of her on the way back?"

She sighed despondently, "Not voluntarily. I was able to pick up a few scenes that she kept replaying in her head. Mostly it was Alex and Katie in the bar being very affectionate with each other."

"This isn't just jealousy. Could he have turned Katie?"

"I don't know. I'm sorry, Michael."

Throwing the phone into the woods sounded like a very good idea at that point. Instead, I ground my teeth together and tried to regain some control of my rage.

"Michael?"

"Be back before dawn. Isaiah will arrive tomorrow night. We need to be prepared."

Sarah fell asleep eventually. When I lifted her from the seat, her head rolled against my shoulder, and the chill of her skin alarmed me. She was so pale.

Whatever was ailing her, I began to suspect it wasn't just confined to the emotional torture she'd been through recently. When I entered her bedroom, the scent of Alex washed over me. It made me feel physically ill imagining him being in that room.

When I had her stretched out upon her bed, her chest rising and falling with shallow little breaths that seemed frighteningly insufficient for a human, I covered her with her bedclothes and rushed downstairs. In the library, I found what I was looking for. Sarah's personal address book.

There was only one thought in my mind as I dialed the doctor's phone number. I had to try to stop whatever was happening inside her body. The virus or infection must be destroyed. And Fleming seemed the most likely person to lend assistance.

"This is Doctor Fleming." He sounded bleary with sleep. I felt somewhat pleased at having awakened him.

"This is Michael. Sarah is ill. You must come out here immediately."

I heard him fumble with his eyeglasses, "What's wrong with her?"

"I was hoping you might be able to tell me. Her breathing is off. Too quick and light. She's cold to the touch and hasn't been acting like herself for hours. Too quiet."

"Has she been bitten?" I was expecting this line of questioning.

"Yes. Several times. It was Alex."

"I'll be there directly."

I was waiting by one of the windows when his headlights slashed through the darkness like dull silver knives. The fear that had been churning through me at the notion of Sarah's possible demise had become a tangle of lead in my veins. It weighed me down, pulling me into despair so unfamiliar and strange to me that I had no idea how to move or think.

Nothing in my long years on this God-forsaken earth had prepared me for such disillusion, such contemptible helplessness. I'd known loss first hand, though I had learned to toss my head at it and shrug it all off after a short period of time. As a human, I'd seen and felt with the subdued sensations of that species the aching and weeping that inevitably followed the death of a loved one. My mother's death had been a particularly bleak instance in my human life all those centuries ago.

However, with the supernatural height of all senses that vampires must experience in the world, not once had I ever been so attached to a human being that I felt true fear at the loss of one from my life. I became convinced that if Sarah should truly die, it would be the end of me. This realization was singularly stunning in its sense of finality. How odd it was to see my travels and attachments coming to such an abrupt and pointless ending.

So I decided that something, anything must be done to save Sarah's life.

The doctor was quick to get started. He hurried up to her room, peered at her closely, withdrew several instruments from his black bag and set out to determine what might be the cause of her malady. He inquired about the bites from Alex, when they might have occurred and the sites of each on her utterly pale, clammy skin.

"What is wrong with her?"

He shook his head, withdrew his stethoscope from his neck, and looked at me gravely. "His venom. It's taken root in her bloodstream. We need something to counteract the effects."

"My venom?"

"If you sealed the wounds Alex made, then your venom is already there." He smoothed back a stray lock of her dark hair, wet with perspiration. His eyes looked upon her with weary resolution.

"What about blood?" The dreadful idea of that proposition made me shiver, even as I uttered the words.

"Perhaps Alex's blood might reverse the effects." He replied doubtfully.

"No. I'm sure she'd rather die than face what dangers that might bring her."

The doctor wasn't hopeful. I could easily discern the defeat that blanketed his whole body. My thoughts were scattered. Who else had the kind of venom that might obliterate this horrible thing that was happening to her? Before the question came to my lips, I knew the answer.

Isaiah. He would be highly amused by this turn of events in his favor. I could imagine the victorious flash in those grey eyes, the scornful words that would likely pour forth like salt on the wounds of my pride. But it was the most likely solution. I would have to rid myself of the antagonism I felt for that horrid old creature in order to save the woman who lay so still before me on that bed.

Ignoring the quiet impotent presence of the doctor, I sat by her side and gathered her still form up against me. Her breathing had grown ragged, echoing brokenly through her. She moaned very quietly, her breath hot through the thin shirt I wore. I wanted to be in her veins, fighting it out of her myself, making real use of all the rage that had consumed me over the preceding hours.

I kissed her softly on the forehead.

"We think there's a way to save you, my love. It won't be pleasant, but there's a chance at least." I spoke these words with the reverence and severity of a man in love. Perhaps that was exactly it. There wasn't nearly enough time to peruse the matter at all. All that mattered to me was that she lived. Later I might have the leisure to sort through the emotional turmoil of it.

Turning to the doctor, I addressed him calmly, "Call Katie on her cell phone. Explain the situation. Ask her to come as quickly as she can. I think I know how to save Sarah's life, but if it all goes to hell, she should have her sister here with her."

CHAPTER 17 - SARAH

The physical pain had become more than just a mild annoyance, but it was still nothing in comparison to the dreadful guilt that squeezed itself into every tiny cell of my body. I couldn't seem to move away from it. Katie was suffering because of me. Though she may have had no conscious realization of it, her dreams could come crashing down around her once she realized what she was to become. I felt only a small hint of doubt that my sister would become a vampire after what I'd seen between her and Alex.

My body felt numb in most places. My fingertips tingled but afforded no real sensation of touch against anything, although I felt sure that I was in my own bed. My ears picked up some distinct sounds, but they faded in and out like a radio being tuned back and forth to different stations.

"...blood...Katie."

The sounds grew fainter. Then I heard nothing and could see nothing. Blackness engulfed me from all sides, but the expected rise of panic did not come. I was simply floating along on a tide of uncertainty, wondering if there would be some divine light at the end of my meandering and hoping that wherever I ended up, I would find myself secure in Michael's embrace.

CHAPTER 18 - MICHAEL

The doctor had done as he was bid. He called Katie on her cell phone and had explained that Sarah seemed very sick and that it would be a good idea to come home as soon as she could. Whatever the girl's response, it was done. If she came or not, it mattered little to me. If Alex came with her, I would not be able to kill him, though my heart cried out for such revenge.

Victoria and Jones returned an hour before dawn. They did not arrive alone. Meekah's slim figure, dressed exquisitely in a cool sky-blue linen traveling suit, appeared behind Jones when I met them at the boundary of the containment field. With Sarah unable to give permission for the three of them to enter, nor for myself to leave, we seemed to be at an impasse.

The doctor had remained back at the house with Sarah, so it was up to me to explain what was happening. Victoria's expression went from mildly worried to full-blown sadness in just a few minutes.

Halfway through my commentary, Meekah held up one heavily jeweled hand to speak.

"The doctor has been in contact with Isaiah."

"That wouldn't surprise me." I grumbled.

Victoria nodded firmly, "He is probably on his way here now. How do you want to handle this, Michael?"

A deep sigh issued forth from Jones, "You'll not be letting that woman go, will you, mate?"

"Not for anything, Jones. Not while it's in my power to save her."

There was a rustle of wind and movement near us in the trees, and I sensed at once that Sarah's murderer was close at hand. But it was the form of a lithe young woman who leapt down to the ground before us all.

"Katie." I nodded at her cautiously. She appeared to be in the throes of the change. There was a brightness to her eyes and skin that hadn't existed the last time I'd seen her. She moved with a different kind of purpose, an unconscious grace that spoke volumes about what she might soon become.

She wasted not a moment on pleasantries, but came right to the point with hands on her slender hips and her dark eyes narrowed.

"Is Sarah any better?"

"No. She's rather worse than she was, actually. You might thank your new boyfriend for that." I replied coldly as the others stared at her.

She laughed. "He's hardly my boyfriend. Why are you all standing here?"

"An invitation is necessary, girl." Meekah said.

"Oh," She rolled her eyes. "Well, come on then. All of you."

Victoria glanced at her uneasily. Jones shifted his weight and crossed his arms.

Katie looked back at us over her shoulder, a roguish smile tinged with bitterness on her pretty face, "Relax, bloodsuckers. I've as much right as Sarah to hand out invitations here."

Meekah's dark eyebrows rose slightly and she shrugged, stepping forward. As she met no resistance, she turned back to Victoria and Jones, "It's all good, lovebirds."

It was a silent walk to that big house. Not a word was spoken between the five of us as we approached it. Alex was nearby. I could smell the fiend all around us. It occurred to me that he might go straight to

Sarah inside the house, but the moment my suspicions became aroused, Victoria reached out with one of her tiny cold hands and squeezed my arm. It was a signal we'd used in the past. She was asking me to wait.

Sadie came bounding down from the front porch at the first sight of Katie, but stopped abruptly once she got caught the new scent of her former mistress. The dog whined, looked around at all of us in a desperate moment of confusion, and then tucked her tail between her legs and retreated towards the barn.

"Katie, what has happened between you and Alex?" Victoria's question was innocently uttered, as not to provoke the girl. We were making our way up the stairs to the porch.

When the girl turned to answer, there was fire in her eyes. Whether it was directed towards Victoria or the situation in which she'd found herself was yet unclear, but the tone of her voice was increasingly self-depreciating.

"I've been used as a pawn, if you have to ask. I thought you could read minds or something."

"Not always and certainly not just bloody anyone." Jones said.

As Katie, Jones and Meekah ascended the stairs to see how Sarah was doing, I pulled Victoria aside and into the kitchen, where only the light above the sink had been left to ward off the inky black night through the first floor of the house.

"What is in the doctor's head?" I urged as quietly as I could.

"He's spoken to Isaiah and urged him to come early. There's no malice there, Michael. The man is genuinely concerned about Sarah."

"So Isaiah is our only hope for her?"

She nodded briskly, "As far as he knows, yes."

"What about Alex? Any idea what he has planned?"

Her gaze lowered to the floor, and I watched the doubt wash over her face.

"He's in agony. He hates himself for what he's done. He loves Sarah desperately and wants her to get well. Katie has been released from his compulsion." She finished with a slow shake of her head, "There's so much pain here, Michael."

"Indeed. Unfortunately, I think we've all had a hand in it in our own way." I admitted with no small amount of consternation.

Katie swept in, her face a mix of horror of anguish, tears tracing down her cheeks like little rivers, "She's going to die, isn't she?" She turned to me with hooded eyes that were heavy with her own internal suffering.

"Did the doctor tell you about Isaiah?" I asked.

"He only said that there was a vampire coming here whose venom may be able to save her. But it's no sure thing, is it? What if it doesn't work? Will you turn her into a vampire?"

From the corner of my eye, I caught movement. Someone had moved into the kitchen from the dining room. When I fully turned my head to see, Alex was standing there. He didn't move closer to the others or me. He seemed unsure of himself.

"Please don't turn her." His tone was shallow and haunted. He looked like a man who was about to lose everything. Meekah had come in from the entryway by the stairs and looked upon Alex with unveiled wonder.

He returned her stare with a blank look, "I'm sorry for what I've done. More sorry than you can imagine. If she dies because of me, you have every right in the world to destroy me. I'll beg you to do it. But don't turn Sarah into one of us. She'd grow to hate herself, and everything we all adore about her will be lost forever."

"Isaiah is at the boundary." Victoria whispered, "I can feel him there."

"Anyone with him?"

It was Meekah who answered, "Six guards..." She closed her eyes, and her head turned one way and then another, the slender neck and jaw firm with her abundant pride in her ability, "And there's an old woman and a young man. He's dark. Straight black hair pulled back."

Katie hurried towards the front door and called over her shoulder, "Sarah can't wait much longer. I'm bringing them up here."

"No need." Said Victoria slowly, "They've come through the boundary."

Every pair of eyes in the room became fixed on her in absolute astonishment. Katie took a few hesitant steps towards Victoria, "But how..."

"The young man with them is a Pawnee." Meekah said roughly.

CHAPTER 19 - SARAH

During rare moments of mental clarity, I could feel an increasing pain in my chest that made me want to scream. My heart felt like it was being gripped by a ruthlessly hard hand, squeezing and kneading the organ with endless brutality. It gave me cause to forget about the guilt. I could hear my own voice rise in pathetic moans and feel the waves of pain move from my chest down through my abdomen and legs.

When I had contemplated death in the past, it had never occurred to me that the pain would be this severe. But surely, death was the dark thing coming for me. Whatever the mysterious cause, whatever the dastardly reason for it all, I was bound to take my last breath very soon.

A release from the pain seemed a glorious thing in those moments. If I should never see the sun sending down warmth and brilliant light upon my home again, it did not matter. If I should never again set my gaze upon the blindingly white snow in the hills of Brown County, it mattered even less. However, there was still a responsibility left to me that I must continue to shoulder and drag on. It had to be carried forward.

With that one clear thought branded upon my suffering body, I gathered every fragment of strength and reserve left to me and vowed to fight the pain. Whatever this thing was that had invaded me and tried to take over, I was dead set against letting it win.

CHAPTER 20 - MICHAEL

The old clock on the fireplace mantle was just striking seven o'clock when we stepped out of the house to meet them. I fumbled in my jacket pocket for the crystal Victoria had given me. It would be essential to have it handy once the sun came up.

When we stepped out onto the porch, we observed the group before us with trepidation. Isaiah, tall and imposingly stern with a violently victorious expression shining in his eyes, was accompanied by a half dozen guards. Each of them was an experienced fighter and had proven their allegiance to Isaiah and the council repeatedly. Next to Isaiah stood a figure very familiar to me, having been tutored extensively under her gentle ministrations when I first became a vampire.

Theodora had not changed at all in my sight. She still walked and spoke like a queen, which was entirely appropriate considering her position in the world back when she was human. She nodded at me formally with only the hint of a smile showing.

The young man standing on the other side of Isaiah was a mystery, to be sure. He was well over six feet tall, lean and powerful with silky dark hair swept back away from his face and tied at the nape of his neck. He was undoubtedly Native American, judging by the classic brow and straight nose, as well as the coffee color of his eyes. Although, when I studied him more thoroughly, I realized that he was looking at nothing. He was unreachable.

Gesturing at the native, I addressed Isaiah in a curt tone, "Compulsion is a bit of a low trick for you, Isaiah. Surely you realized we had to let you into the containment field in order to get this business done."

"Well, I find it's always prudent to have a plan B." He said while brushing a bit of lint off his wool coat with a gloved fingertip. He looked over our group, tilted his head minutely and smiled.

"So where is Alexander? I'm very anxious to meet this extraordinary young man."

Katie sighed, "We don't have time for this."

Teddy spoke up suddenly, her eyes portraying the worry that she carried, "She's right. Let's do what we can for Sarah, and then we can all hopefully sit down and have a meeting of the minds."

Isaiah's eyebrows went up, "Is the girl truly at death's door?"

"She is. Your venom may be powerful enough to reverse the damage." Katie said.

We all heard the front door open and close. As we all turned, we saw Alex striding towards us with Sarah in his arms, limp and nearly lifeless. His face was set in fearless determination as he approached Isaiah and carefully laid Sarah at his feet like a sleeping child.

"*Do it now.*" Alex commanded.

The older vampire gave him a disdainful glance before looking over at me, "We haven't discussed the terms of our arrangement."

"Isaiah..." Teddy crossed her arms, "This young woman may die right here if you don't help."

I moved to stand at Alex's side and met Isaiah eye-to-eye, "What do you want from me?"

"Surrender your blood."

I heard a gasp from behind me that sounded like Victoria. Jones growled in protest at the suggestion. It was then that Meekah slid up to Alex's other side and urged him to take a few steps back. A whispered conversation began between Alex, Meekah and Victoria. Ordinarily, I would have no trouble hearing it, but with Sarah laying there on the ground about to die unless I gave myself up to Isaiah, I didn't feel the need to pay much attention. I should have.

"Well, Michael? Do you feel strongly enough about this human to hand yourself over?"

Gazing down upon the face of the woman I was about to sacrifice myself for, I felt such a rush of tenderness flow through me that I feared I might weep. I couldn't do such a thing before these people, so I pushed back against the emotional tide as forcefully as I could and merely nodded my consent.

Of all the bloody battles I'd fought and all the needless blood I had spilled, I felt at that moment a measure of remorse. Perhaps this act would be my redemption. I doubted it would cover all my sins.

A feral smile rolled across Isaiah's bearded face before he lowered himself towards Sarah with his fangs extended. I couldn't watch it. Instead, I stared at the trees and the pale landscape around me. Even when Sarah groaned in protest at being bitten by this stranger, I did not look at the two of them.

The conversation that had been going on behind me suddenly erupted into shouts. I noticed that the young Pawnee man had begun to look vaguely uncomfortable. Why had he come into the containment field? He could have remained at the border to let them out again once this was over. Apparently, he had another purpose for being there.

Whatever had been said between Alex and the two women had enraged him sorely. When Isaiah stood again and patted at his mouth with a square white handkerchief, Alex had come back to stand by me with fury rolling off him like a storm cloud.

"Why is this Indian here?" Alex barked out sharply towards Isaiah.

"Alex, is it?"

"Yes. Now answer the question!"

Ignoring the two of them, I bent down to examine Sarah. She was still pale as a sheet, but her eyelids were fluttering against her cheeks, and she was trying to lift her hands to her head. I slipped one arm under legs and another beneath her back and lifted her. I wasn't about to leave her between those two idiots while they argued.

I was halfway up the porch steps when I heard Alex's accusation.

"He's here to get her pregnant, isn't he? To continue the precious line and preserve the containment field!"

I heard an unnatural crackle of power behind me as Alex's rage grew. All I knew was that I had to get Sarah out of the way. I'd deal with Isaiah and his schemes later. As I propped the door open with one shoulder and turned to go through the doorway sideways with Sarah, I looked over to see what was happening.

The Indian had disappeared. I didn't see Theodora anywhere either. Bursts of brightness were flying from Alex's fingers, gliding swiftly through the air and dispatching Isaiah's guards one by one, leaving them lifeless on the ground with black burn marks peppered across different parts of their bodies. One ball of fire missed its mark and flew onward into the forest.

Isaiah, desperate to save his own life, had grabbed Katie and darted down towards the road with her. Alex did not follow, but fell to his knees in the grass, weak from the amount of power he'd expended. Jones went after them, followed by Victoria. I knew they'd never catch them before they hit the boundary. And Isaiah had the only means of getting out with Katie as his prisoner.

I swept Sarah into the house and up the stairs. I laid her carefully on her own bed and checked her pulse with my fingertips. It was much stronger than it had been. When I pulled the top sheet over her, she smiled faintly and turned her head into her pillow to lay on her side.

The morning sun was just beginning to penetrate through the branches of the trees around the house, and the light glimmered through her bedrooms windows like something from a beautiful dream. I longed to settle down next to her on the bed and hold her for the rest of the day. But there was work to do.

Leaning down, I kissed her cheek and turned to leave.

S.J. Wright

CHAPTER 21 - SARAH

When I opened my eyes, it seemed wrong that everything was so dark. My body felt rested and relaxed, although my stomach felt a little queasy. I reached over to the lamp on my nightstand and switched it on.

Sadie was at my side in an instant, licking my fingers and nudging me gently.

"Hey, pretty girl." I said, laughing lightly.

I swung my legs over the side of the bed and stood up. Everything was so quiet. The only sound was Sadie's nails clicking against the wood floor in my bedroom. When I opened the bedroom door and looked down the hall, I saw a crack of light on the floor under Katie's bedroom door. Sadie slipped by me and headed downstairs.

Trying to be as quiet as possible, I tiptoed down to Katie's door. Inside, I heard two familiar voices.

"You're lucky you got away from him." Alex said quietly.

A huff of impatience followed, "Lucky? The bastard bit me. Now I'm probably going to turn into a freaking bloodsucker."

"Katie, that won't happen. I know it feels like it, but as long as you don't drink any more blood, you should be fine."

Any *more* blood? I shuddered and pressed my ear closer to the door.

"It's a little addictive, you know?"

"Yeah, but you're way too close to changing. No more blood. Ever."

"Yes, fine. I get it."

So she had been drinking Alex's blood? Voluntarily? I backed away from the door and went back into my own bedroom. Confusion swirled through me. What had I missed? The last thing I remembered was Victoria driving me home after the meeting with Teddy. There was a little memory of seeing Alex downtown, but I wasn't sure that hadn't been a dream or something.

Where was Michael?

I went back into my room, shut the door slowly, and sat down on my bed. Something was really messed up around here. Then I heard an odd noise from my bedroom closet. A rustle of something moving. That was a little strange.

When I opened up the closet door, there was a man standing there. A stranger. He was tall with straight brown hair that was long enough to brush his shoulders. His eyes were wide with fear when he saw me. I hopped back in surprise and landed on my bed.

"I'm sorry." He said slowly, seeming to struggle with each word.

"Who are you?"

He moved towards me with a terribly sad expression on his face, "I'm so sorry. They told me I had to do it."

Backing up, I scrambled onto the other side of the bed.

"Who are you? What are you apologizing for?" I asked, beginning to feel some real fear moving through me again.

He was on me before I even put up much of a struggle, holding one hand over my mouth to stop me from screaming.

"They said I had to do it. I'm so sorry."

He was weeping, the hot tears falling on my stomach as he wrenched my pants and underwear down to my ankles. The door flew open a moment later, and before Alex could hold her back, my sister attacked the man who was holding me down.

We knew the moment she stepped over the line and tasted his blood. Her eyes grew incredibly wide and she shoved the stranger away from her. I stared at my sister and found it hard to draw a breath.

"Oh no, Katie…" Alex whispered.